I0668868

Tales of the Wild West
Volume Four

Airship 27 Productions

The Masked Rider: Tales of the Wild West Volume Four

"The Ghost Town Oulaws" © 2024 John Rose
"Wild Duck" and "The Alamo Reflex" © 2024 Alan J. Porter
"Masterson's Gamble © 2024 Teel James Glenn
"A World Aflame" © 2024 George Tackes

An Airship 27 Production
Airship27.com
Airship27Hangar.com

Interior and cover illustrations ©2024 Shannon Hall

Editor: Ron Fortier
Associate Editor: Gordon Dymowski
Marketing and Promotions Manager: Michael Vance
Production designer: Rob Davis

All rights reserved under International and Pan-American Copyright Conventions. No part of this book may be reproduced in any manner without permission in writing from the copyright holder, except by a reviewer, who may quote brief passages in a review.

ISBN: 978-1-953589-94-1

Published in the United States of America

10 9 8 7 6 5 4 3 2 1

TABLE OF CONTENTS

THE MASKED RIDER

"Ghost Town Outlaws"

by John Rose

oonlight shimmered from the huge boulders lining the trail leading toward Red Rock City, some five miles beyond the ridge. The night air was clear and crisp. Above, the bright stars created numerous dark and light patches along the slope.

A shadowy form came into view, angling down the side and away from the clump of trees a short distance above the road. The shape would disappear and reappear as the rider passed through the dark patches and around clumps of yucca and sagebrush.

Then a second and third shape appeared. One was a rider and the other one was a pack horse that followed without a lead rope. He was well trained and did not linger far behind his companion.

The first rider came to a stop along the side of the road, listening. In the distance could be heard the sounds of an approaching vehicle.

"*Senor*, that sounds like wagon coming very fast," commented the lean Mexican Indian as he drew his gray up beside the first rider. "Maybe runaway, you think?"

"Yep, sounds like it," the dark clad man said. Immediately he began removing the black mask and the *mantilla* from his shoulders. As he was doing this, his companion moved into the shadows along with the pack horse. There he would remain unseen unless it became necessary that he take part in whatever happened.

The first rider, astride a sleek black stallion, folded the silk material forming the mask and the *mantilla* he had been wearing. These he placed in the saddle bags tied behind the cantle of his saddle. The man was dressed in black shirt and trousers with black boots and *sombrero*. There was nothing shiny or ornamental about his outfit. Even the saddle was completely black.

"Easy, Midnight, easy," he spoke soothingly to the horse. The animal was beginning to fidget as he, too, was hearing the sound of the approaching wagon.

"Steady, boy," the man continued speaking softly to the horse. "Makes you wonder just what someone is doing out at this time of night and racing their horses like that," he said. "But I guess we'll soon know," he added as the buckboard came careening around the bend in the road.

The horses were lathered and pulling hard. The left horse seemed to be fighting against the pull of the reins, while his teammate was running free and easy, although frightened.

The driver was pulling hard against the reins from the left horse, causing the animal to turn his head back somewhat with the pressure. There seemed to be no connection between the driver and the right hand horse.

The dark clad man gigged his horse into motion and quickly they were running along the side of the road. As the runaway team drew even, the cowboy reached over and caught the bridle of the horse on the right hand side. Steadily Midnight slowed while his rider maintained a strong grip on the harness.

Soon the wagon was slowed to a trot with the team blowing and breathing deeply. When they came to a stop, the dark rider dismounted but continued to hold the headstall of the horse.

"Thanks, mister!" came a feminine voice. "You came along just at the right time!"

"Seems like you don't have reins to this sorrel horse," came the reply from the man as he looked back at the driver.

"Nope," the woman replied. "When I put some pressure into trying to control the team, they just popped!" The driver had set the brake and climbed down to join the man.

"Right here," he said, showing her the stub of the remaining rein, "looks like it was cut. Maybe just partly, so it would break when someone reared back on it. The other one was sliced the same way."

"Yeah, it does look that way," the woman agreed, looking at the smooth cut. Then she looked up at the tall man's face. "I don't recognize you," she said. "You're not from around here, are you?"

"No, I'm just ridin' through," he smiled. "Name is Wade Morgan. Might I ask how come you are out here with a wagon this late? It is almost midnight."

"Sure, you can ask," she smiled, "and I have a very good answer. We had a church social in Red Rock this evening. I was on the committee, so was involved in cleaning up afterwards. That explains the night time drive. However, it doesn't explain why my team was running away like they were."

"No, it doesn't," agreed Morgan. "And it doesn't explain why your reins were cut."

"I'm from the CR Bar Ranch," she explained. "And was heading back that way when someone near the road fired a number of shots. I never saw anyone but they were very close to the roadway. That's what spooked the horses. Then when I tried to rein them in, the lines to Red just broke."

"Maybe we'd better check and see if either horse is suffering from a bullet wound," said the dark rider. "They may have actually been shooting at you. But you say you never saw anyone?"

"No," the blonde woman said, shaking her head. "I had the feeling there was more than one person shooting, but I don't know that. Oh, Mr. Morgan, my name is Nellie Robertson. My father is Charles Robertson of the CR Bar."

"Nice to meet you, Nellie," the tall stranger said and held out his hand. "And just call me Wade." He was a little surprised at the solid handshake from the young woman. It told him she was no stranger to work.

"Wade," she said, "you may have been a much greater help to me than you realize. Not far from here is the turn to head out to the CR Bar. It is a rather sharp turn off the road and if these horses were still going crazy, like they were, I believe they would have rolled the buckboard. I would have been in it and they were harnessed to it."

"That could have been really bad," nodded Morgan. "Now, I can fix those reins so that you can get on out to the ranch," he added, "but, of course, someone will need to do it properly before you use the harness again. But I am wondering if these horses are going to be settled down enough for you to drive?"

"I think they are," the girl said. "They are generally a very good team. That's how come Dad let's me drive them. It was just those gunshots that spooked them."

The young woman went to the wagon and retrieved the lines for Red, which she had dropped on the floor of the wagon when they snapped. She handed them to the stranger.

A short time later, Wade Morgan had the reins reattached to the harness. "These knots will hold," he said to Nellie, "but don't try to keep using it with just the knots holding them in place. You'd likely find yourself without control of your team again."

"Yes, I'll get Whop to fix it," the girl said. "He's our foreman, Whop Dunbar, and he is good at fixing things like this."

"Good. Now let me check this sorrel. He's been pretty antsy while I reattached the rein, but I'm wondering if he might have been grazed by a bullet. I think we should take a look."

Nellie held the headstall to control the movement while the stranger began running his hands over the animal, looking for anything that might indicate the horse had been snipped by a bullet. He started at the head and worked his way back. When he was near the hind quarters, the horse began moving around, trying to keep his rump away from the man.

"Right here," said Morgan, indicating a spot on the horse's rump, "there is a place that looks like it might be where a bullet grazed him. He certainly doesn't want me to touch it."

"I'll let somebody know when I get back to the ranch," said Nellie. "They can do whatever needs to be done."

"Okay. I'll ride with you to the turn, then I'll be on my way."

"Are you going to be around Red Rock for a while?" the girl asked. "Maybe I'll see you again, if you are."

Wade Morgan shrugged. "Hard to say."

"Hey, you wouldn't be looking for a job, would you? Dad would probably hire you, especially if I put in a good word. Interested?"

"Actually, I'm just riding through, but I may stay around Red Rock for a few days. If I feel the need for a job, I just might ride out to your ranch."

Nellie drove the buckboard to the turn-off for the CR Bar. She slowed the team and looked over at the tall stranger.

"Ranch is about two miles that way," she called out, pointing to the southwest.

The man nodded and raised his hand to his hat brim.

The young woman clucked to her horses and they trotted toward the ranch.

Dawn was breaking and the Yaqui Indian, taller than his people who were a notably tall tribe, was adjusting the pack on the sorrel horse known as Slow Joe. The name had nothing to do with the speed of the animal and Wade Morgan would, on occasion, ride the red horse in lieu of the big black Midnight.

"*Senor*," said the native, looking over the back of Pretty Boy, his saddled gray horse, "do you plan to stay in Red Rock for a while? Or do we move on?"

"Blue Hawk," said the Masked Rider, still dressed as Wade Morgan, "I've been thinking and I believe we'll spend a little time here. The horses could use the rest and time to just graze."

"Huh," the Indian replied. "That girl with the yellow hair was pretty, was she not?"

"Yep, she was kind of a looker," the Masked Rider admitted.

"Maybe you want to stay around and maybe see this woman again?" Blue Hawk suggested with the trace of a smile on his face.

"Could never do that, my friend," the tall man replied, grinning. "There is nothing I can offer a woman. That is, unless she wants to ride the owl-hoot trail with us."

Blue Hawk chuckled softly. "*Senor*, no woman wants to be an outlaw."

"Yeah," agreed the man known as Wade Morgan. "I figured we'd ride into Red Rock this morning and do a little listening. I can't figure why someone would cut the reins to a team of horses and then spook them into running away. It may have just been a prank of some kind. If we can't come up with something a little more realistic, we'll just ride on. There is no point in getting involved in something that will work itself out with time. Besides, I'd kind of like to get a real meal at a cafe."

"Huh. I not like cafe so much. Give me fresh meat and a fire and I be happy."

"You must be happy most of the time," nodded the man as he fastened the cinch on Midnight's saddle. "That is pretty much our steady diet, my friend."

Blue Hawk nodded silently and mounted his dapple gray. He turned toward the pack horse and gave a low twittering whistle. The animal's head came up and he ambled over to join the riders.

"You go into Red Rock first," said Blue Hawk. "I will be along with Pretty Boy and Slow Joe after while."

Blue Hawk, the Yaqui Indian from Mexico, had been educated in a mission school and could speak excellent English when he chose to do so. He could also read and write both English and Spanish. He was middle aged and like many of his people, it was difficult to tell whether he was twenty-five or perhaps fifty-five years of age. He chose to ride with the Masked Rider and they were very close friends.

Wade Morgan was a name adopted by the tall man long ago and no one knew for sure just where he came from or what had prompted him to become the Masked Rider. At times he was referred to as the Robin Hood Outlaw, but most of the time he was wanted as a desperado with a price on his head. As such, he was careful about being associated with Blue Hawk and when he was in the guise of Wade Morgan, he was just a simple cowpuncher moving through the west.

Morgan lately had been wondering if it were time for him to just completely disappear. Perhaps move far away from the west, marry, settle down with a family and let the Masked Rider become a thing of the past. It sounded tempting, as he rode that morning toward the sleepy western settlement of Red Rock, but he knew he could not make it last. There was something about him, wanderlust, if you will, that kept him moving. Moving and looking for those situations where the law needed help, help from outside the law! That was where the Masked Rider fit into the scheme of things. He could bring justice to those the law couldn't touch! This, of course, made the Masked Rider an outlaw!

Blue Hawk and Morgan had moved to a spot where there was water, the previous night. There they started a small fire, heated a pot of coffee and relaxed. A short time later they were stretched out on their bedrolls and sleeping lightly. The coffee did not affect either man as far as the ability to go to sleep after drinking it.

The tall man felt good that morning as he rode Midnight toward Red Rock City. He had let the big black gallop most of the way as he wanted to put some distance between himself and the Indian. They did not want anyone to see them arrive close together and suspicion they were companions.

They were still several miles outside of Red Rock and Morgan was wondering if the spooked horses had actually ran wildly all that distance to the point where he had stopped them. Perhaps they had, since Nellie had only one horse that she could control and the buckboard was fairly light with no load of any kind, other than the driver's weight.

As he rode, Morgan also kept a sharp watch on the trail, or road, he was following. When he found the spot where the kicked up dirt indicated the woman's horses had broken into a run, he stopped to look around. Because it was the horse on the right side of the team that suffered the graze of a bullet, he moved off the road in that direction to look around. He had a feeling that he should take a look at the area where the gunman had been firing shots. Or two men, if Nellie's thinking was correct.

He rode the big black up the slope, picking their way carefully, looking for a spot that would indicate someone had spent some time there. Midnight gave the first warning that something was not right. The horse blew through his nostrils and pranced sideways.

"Whoa, fellah," the man said soothingly, as he glanced around to see if he could pick out whatever it was that irritated the horse. Then he saw a pair of boots sticking out from the base of a large boulder.

"I think you found it, fellah," he said softly as he dismounted.

Wade Morgan stepped around the rock to find the body of a young man stretched out on the ground, his hat nearby. There was a bloody spot directly in the middle of his chest. The fellow had caught a slug that had killed him rather quickly.

Nellie hadn't mentioned shooting back, but she had said she thought there might have been two shooters. Either she had fired back and scored a lucky hit or there had been two of them and, for some reason, one had decided to shoot the other one. Believing the second scenario being the most plausible, Morgan began searching the area. Presently he found a second set of tracks and followed them over the ridge. Just below the summit, on the back side, there was indication two horses had been tied there. The man on foot had mounted one and led the other one as he left.

Retracing his steps, Morgan stopped by the corpse just long enough to check the six-gun that lay beside the body. Every shot had been fired. The gun was empty. If the second man planned to shoot his companion, he most likely kept track of the shots. When the first shooter's gun was empty, the second fellow had just simply shot him. Morgan replaced the gun where it had fallen. He did not check the body for identification as there likely would not have been any. He was also reluctant to disturb anything. Gun, hat and body all remained exactly as he had found them.

Morgan slowed his black to a walk as they entered town. He remained very observant as they walked along the dusty main street. They had passed a livery stable at the edge of town with a small pasture located behind it. Then there was a harness shop and a blacksmith shop located across the street from each other. The Buttermilk Cafe was beside a dress shop. Then came a telegraph office and across the street was the Golden Nugget Saloon, although Wade

Morgan doubted there had ever been any gold discovered in this part of the country. There was a mercantile store, a general store, a hotel, a wagon shop, a feed store, another livery stable and a second saloon, The Red Eagle. There were various other businesses spread along the main street. Near the center of town was the Sheriff's office with the jail directly behind it. The two buildings were attached.

He drew Midnight to a stop at the office. The door seemed to be locked and he decided that the sheriff probably had not arrived as yet. He was turning back toward his horse when he saw a man hurrying toward him. It appeared that he could have come from the Golden Nugget.

"Bet that might be the lawman," he said softly to Midnight. He waited as the fellow approached.

"Morning!" the man called. "You be needing me for something?"

"Howdy," Morgan replied. "Would you be the sheriff?"

"Yep! Got something on your mind?"

Morgan nodded. "Yeah, I do. Let's step inside and I'll tell you what I know and then you can do whatever you see fit."

The Sheriff unlocked the door and they went into the cool interior.

"My name is Wade Morgan and I am just passing through."

"I'm Sheriff Locke," the man said. "Call me Jim, if you like."

"Nice to meet you," Morgan reached out to shake hands. The thought crossed his mind that a great many sheriffs would not have shaken hands as it would have put them in a bind for drawing their own gun.

"Okay, what's the problem?"

"First, I need to ask you a question. Just something to settle a doubt in my own mind. Was there some kind of social event at the church last evening?"

"Yeah, I think so," the law officer replied. "I didn't go because that is the time when trouble is most likely to break out in the saloons."

"Makes sense." Morgan pulled up a chair and sat down. Jim Locke sat down behind his desk.

"Now, I want to ask you a question," said Sheriff Locke. "You are wearing two pistols and have them tied down. Are you a gunman?"

"No, sir. I do not consider myself one. I can use the guns, either right handed or left handed. I do not look for gun fights as some gun slicks do, nor do I wear them for show. I have nothing to prove and the longer they can stay pouched, the happier I am."

The sheriff smiled. "That's good to know. Now, what exactly brings you to see me?"

"Here's the story," Morgan said and proceeded to tell the lawman about stopping the runaway team, the cut reins, Nellie's story about being shot at and how he had stopped and looked around at the point where the horses had been frightened into running. When he told the lawman about finding the body of a young man, the officer became very interested.

"As you can tell, Mr. Morgan, I am not very old to be holding down the office of sheriff. The chances are if this dead fellow was from around here, I probably grew up with him!"

The sheriff asked many questions and Wade Morgan answered them to the best of his knowledge. One that he asked, that also interested Morgan, was if he knew if Nellie had fired back at her assailants.

"I don't know," Morgan answered honestly. "I do know that Nellie was wearing a six-gun around her waist and I did think it was unusual for having just been at a church function. But at that time I did not know there would be a dead man involved."

"Yeah, well, that's alright," said Sheriff Locke standing up. "It really ought to be a law officer that asks her that question. Would you like to ride out and show me just where this body is located?"

"I'd rather not, Sheriff. However, I did mark the spot so you can find it easily. I placed two rocks side by side and then placed a smaller one on top of them. It is on the right hand side of the road, right at the edge. I will be around town for a while, perhaps a couple of days, so you should be able to find me at the hotel should you need me."

"Fine. I'll get a couple of boys and we'll take a wagon out there right away."

"I plan to look the town over, stable my horse and get some breakfast," Morgan offered with a friendly smile. "Been a while since I've had a good meal."

Red Rock consisted of one main street running north and south. There were two streets that intersected the main route and they usually led back to residential buildings spaced farther back from the main thoroughfare. There was a church located off the main street and near the homes.

The town had been laid out not far from a stream called Sweet Water Creek. The stable at the north end of town had a pasture that enclosed a portion of the creek where the grazing horses and mules could get to water. There were several trees along the banks providing shade.

Wade Morgan turned Midnight toward this stable as he was impressed with the grazing available and the water and shade. There was a sign hung on the side of the barn proclaiming it to be the North End Livery.

He had just stepped down from the saddle when an older fellow came out of the barn.

"Howdy, pardner. Somethin' I can do for ya?"

"How much to stable my horse?"

"Two bits a day," the hostler replied. "That includes a helping of grain and unlimited grazing and water out back."

"I'll pay for four days," Morgan agreed handing the fellow a silver dollar. "If I decide to stay longer, I'll let you know. If I leave earlier, the extra is yours."

"Fair enough," the old man replied. "My name's Clem. Want me to stable him now?"

"Yeah, Clem. My name's Wade. Nice to meet you. Give him that helping of grain and when he's finished, turn him out to graze. Now, where would be a good place to get some breakfast?"

"If it were me, I'd go to The Pastry. Jest cause its closest. The Buttermilk is good, too, and if you want a drink this early, either one of the saloons lays out a good helping."

"Does that hotel have a kitchen?"

"Yeah, but you asked for a good place," the old man grinned. "The hotel ain't bad, but the others are all better. Jest my opinion, o' course."

"Thanks.," Morgan turned and started down the street as the livery man took Midnight by the reins and led him into the barn.

Wade Morgan stopped at The Pastry.

"What would you like this morning, stranger?" said the waitress after he had seated himself.

"Oh, coffee, bacon, eggs, biscuits and some potatoes."

"Right," the girl jotted it down. "Be out right quickly and I'll get your coffee immediately. How do you want those eggs done?"

"Stir 'em up," Morgan smiled.

"Scrambled it is," the waitress said and hurried back to the kitchen. She disappeared briefly and then reappeared with a cup and a pot of coffee.

There were other customers in the dining room. They had all already received their orders and none of them appeared to be with anyone else. The room was quiet as they ate.

The coffee was good and Wade Morgan thought if the rest of the meal was as good, he might not eat anywhere else.

When he had finished the meal, he felt like The Pastry was one of the better places he had eaten, but decided he would like to try the others if he stayed in Red Rock that long. He picked up his sombrero and moved up to the counter where he paid the waitress.

"You're a stranger here," the girl commented. "Going to be in town long?"

"Maybe. Just a day or two. Let my horse rest up some."

"I'm Pattie Thompson. My folks own The Pastry and we'd be pleased to have you back again!"

"Thanks, I'm Wade Morgan and I'm really just passing through. But your food was good and I just might be back before I leave."

The waitress handed him his change, then in a voice so low it was barely audible, she asked, "Are you a gun slinger?"

"No," replied Morgan in an equally soft whisper. "I'm just a wondering cow-poke is all. I know how to them if I have to, however, I prefer not to."

The girl smiled and nodded. Morgan touched his hat brim and turned toward the screen door.

"Come again," were the words from the waitress as he stepped outside.

Morgan was unaware, as he walked away from The Pastry, of Pattie Johnson coming to the door and watching where he went. It was soon obvious that the stranger was headed for the hotel. The girl smiled to herself and turned back toward the kitchen.

"I wonder if there' a reason why everyone wants to know if I was a gunslinger?" he murmured to himself as he walked toward the hotel. "If so," he continued thinking alound, "would it be because there is a gun hawk or two here in town? Possibly looking for someone to try out?"

The Starlight Hotel was only a block from The Pastry and Wade Morgan stepped into the lobby, planning to get a room for the next few nights. An exceedingly lean man with thin receding hair stood behind the counter. He looked up as Morgan entered, but did not say anything. After a long look, he went back to work on the book spread out before him.

"Pardon me, but do you have a room available?"

The man looked up from the ledger he was working on. "Who's asking?" he snapped bluntly, evidently miffed that he had to come to a stop.

"The fellow who wants to rent it," Morgan fired back. He didn't like people with bad manners.

"Sign here," said the clerk, turning the register around and flipping a couple of pages. "That'll be a buck a night, unless you're going to stay a week and then it only fifty cents a night."

"I'll take it for a week."

"You a gunman?"

"Nope. Why do you ask?"

"Couple of real gunmen here in town right now," the clerk volunteered. "Might be smart to avoid them, if you can."

"Thanks," Morgan took offered room key with a number four printed on the

tag. He turned and went up the stairs. The room was clean and he liked it immediately. He opened a window and stretched out on the bed. Before he knew it,
he was asleep.

Blue Hawk, riding Pretty Boy with Slow Joe only a few steps behind, was not
all that far behind Wade Morgan. But the Yaqui Indian was in no hurry and he
fell farther behind with each passing minute.

Eventually, he came to the spot in the road where the CR Bar team had
churned up the dirt breaking into a run the previous night. Beside the road was
a sign that Blue Hawk was sure Wade Morgan had placed there.

"Something is here," he said softly, pulling Pretty Boy to a stop. He sat for a
moment, then turned off the road on the opposite side from the tell-tale rocks.
He soon found a gully where he could hide the two horses. Once that was done,
he returned and crossed the road. In one hand he carried a short branch he had
broken off a sage and he used it to brush out his tracks when he crossed the road.
It did not take him long to find the corpse.

Blue Hawk squatted on his haunches and observed the body and the surrounding area for several minutes. Then he stood up and circled the area, looking from different angles. He did not disturb anything.

Then he followed the tracks that left the area. He knew that his friend had
followed them as well, but as he moved he was careful to erase his own prints
while not disturbing those of Wade Morgan. Beyond the ridge, he spent many
minutes following and examining the hoof prints.

Blue Hawk was about finished with his observation of the scene when he
heard voices. He dropped down and moved away from the tracks as he assumed
the voices belonged to those who had been sent out to collect the body. If it
was the sheriff, that man would probably follow the footprints, just as he and
Morgan had done.

The Yaqui lay low, waiting and watching. It was several minutes before he
heard the men coming over the ridge. He could hear their voices as they talked
with one another, but he was too far away to actually understand anything that
was said.

Remaining low and moving slowly, Blue Hawk crossed the ridge a hundred
and fifty yards south of the footprints and the body. Still carrying the sage branch,
he crossed the road and retrieved his horses.

By the time Sheriff Jim Locke and his two helpers returned to load the corpse,
the Indian was long gone from the area.

When Blue Hawk reached the outskirts of Red Rock, he moved away from the road and found a meadow some five hundred yards from the trail and the set-tlement. There he tethered both horses where they could graze. He had watered them when they had crossed Sweet Water Creek earlier.

With the horses cared for, Blue Hawk added a dusty *sombrero* and a *serape* to his dress. He changed his moccasins for a pair of sandals and made his way toward Red Rock.

It was well past noon when a vagabond Mexican trudged into the settlement of Red Rock. He continued walking down the main street, seemingly paying little attention to the activity on either side of him. He passed the Starlight Hotel where Wade Morgan sat in the shade on the front porch. The Mexican went by a few more buildings and then disappeared down an alley.

Morgan stood up and stretched. Then he turned and walked into the lobby of the Starlight. The clerk gave him a quick glance and then proceeded to ignore him.

The tall man with the broad shoulders walked slowly up the stairs to the second floor. Then he hurried quietly down the hallway that led the length of the hotel. The back door was barred so that no one could get in during the night. Morgan simply lifted the bar and set it on the floor leaning it against the wall by the back door. He opened the door and stepped outside on the small landing. There were stair steps against the outside wall running down to ground level in the alley. The man gave a soft tweeting chirp of a bird. He stood there for a moment, then stretching as though he had just stepped outside for a breath of fresh air, turned and reentered the hotel. He moved away from the door and waited.

Presently the door opened and Blue Hawk slipped inside, soundless as always. Morgan led the way to number four and they entered.

"Did you see the body?"

"Yes, *Senor*," the Indian replied. "The man was very young, hardly more than a boy."

"Do you reckon he caught a bullet from Nellie or did his partner do him in?" asked Wade Morgan.

Blue Hawk shook his head. "Hard to say," he replied. "I believe if Nellie had returned fire, she would have said so. But maybe not. I think if his partner shot him, he would have been so close the slug would have gone on through him. I did not turn him over, so maybe it did."

"Might have been a smaller caliber bullet, too."

"Could be," nodded the Yaqui.

"…a vagabond Mexican trudged…down main streat…"

"From the footprints," said Morgan, "it looked like his partner was very young or a very small man."

"Or a woman," added Blue Hawk. "Maybe a fat woman. Tracks were deep."

Wade Morgan gave his friend a quick look. "Yeah, it could have been," he said thoughtfully. "Didn't think of that."

"I followed the horse tracks for a little ways," continued the Indian. "Whoever it was with him took both horses and I am wondering why. Having the dead man's horse would not be a smart thing to do."

"Did you get to follow the tracks far enough to know them?"

"Si. I would recognize them if I should see them again."

"Okay. I think I shall go back and talk with Sheriff Locke. I'd like to know what he thinks and if he knew the dead fellow. When business picks up in the saloons, I may go in and see if I can hear anything."

Blue Hawk nodded. "I will return to the street and listen, *Senor*."

Quietly they went to the back door on the second level and the Yaqui Indian slipped out. Wade Morgan watched him from inside the doorway until he was gone. Then he replaced the bar on the door.

When Morgan showed up at the Sheriff's office, it appeared to be empty. The door was open slightly, but no one was inside. He turned to walk away, thinking he would spend some time in one of the saloons and try again later. Then he saw Jim Locke coming across the street, waving at him. He waited.

"How'd it go this morning?" Morgan asked.

"About as easy as I've ever found a body," the sheriff replied. "You had it marked very well and yet not something anyone else would pay much attention to. Come on in."

The sheriff led the way into the office and sat down behind his desk. Morgan pulled up the same chair he had sat in earlier.

"What did you think, Jim? Was it someone you knew?"

"Yeah, I knew him, but he didn't grow up around here. Went by the name of Red Hobin. He came in a couple of years ago and got on at one of the ranches. Seems like he has shifted jobs a couple of times. Don't know if he had trouble getting along with people or if he was just lazy and got let go."

"I assume 'Red' was not his given name, but just a nickname that stuck with him," mused Morgan. "When you loaded the body, did you notice if the bullet went through the body?"

"No, I didn't," the lawman admitted. "The body was pretty stiff and we just covered it up with a horse blanket and loaded it. I usually let the coroner do the checking on the deceased. We could walk over there, if you want?"

"Maybe later. Another thing, did you see or follow the tracks leading away from the corpse? They were rather small, so I assumed it would be a youngster or a small man. I am now wondering if those prints could have been made by a woman or a girl?"

"Huh, hadn't thought of that, Morgan. But it is possible. It would be strange if we had a woman trying to ambush another woman!"

"Did you bring in the dead man's gun?"

"Yeah, I did. Every bullet had been fired."

"So, if his partner is the one who shot him, he just waited until his pistol was empty and the shot him point blank. Being that close, the bullet should have gone all the way through, unless it was a small caliber. If the bullet came from the road, where Nellie was on her buckboard, it might have been far enough away to not go all the way through."

"I see what you are saying," the sheriff scratched his chin. "Do you mind me asking what your interest is in all this? You know, you being a stranger here, and all."

Wade Morgan chuckled. "I guess I would have to say my interest lies in the fact that I stopped Nellie's runaway team last night. That could have ended up really bad for the girl. And she is rather pretty."

Sheriff Locke grinned. "I thought that might be it. But let me tell you, Nellie is around twenty-three or twenty-four years old. I expect she's been asked by older men, maybe a dozen times or more, about getting hitched. She just ain't interested. She has several male friends but none that I would call her steady fellow. Maybe the guy that has the best chance with her would be the CR Bar foreman, Whop Dunbar."

"Well," grinned Morgan, "I really have nothing to offer a woman, so I am not really in the game. I guess I'd just kind of like to see that someone else doesn't take another pot shot at her."

"That makes sense. I think it is about time I rode out and asked a few questions of Nellie Robertson. Would you like to ride along?"

"Yep. I've got my horse up at the North End Livery. It'll take a few minutes to get him saddled and ready."

"Fine. I'll take a quick look-in with the coroner; get my horse and meet you right back here at the office."

The two men went their separate ways. As Wade Morgan headed north, he saw Blue Hawk sitting on a bench in front of The Pastry Cafe. He crossed the street so that he would walk by his friend and at the shop; he stopped, shaded his eyes and looked in the doorway.

"Riding out to the Robertson ranch with the sheriff," he spoke without ever looking at the Mexican sitting silently. Then he turned and walked on.

Unknown to the Morgan, Pattie Thompson saw him look in the door and before she could move to greet him, he had turned away and was walking up the street. She frowned, as she was sure he was looking in to see if she was there. Perhaps he just got cold feet and would wait for another time. She hoped so.

The sheriff and Wade Morgan both arrived back at the office at the same time and they just continued riding south.

"Did the bullet go through the body?" Morgan asked once they were outside of town.

"It did," the sheriff responded. "Didn't leave much of a hole, so we still don't know if he was shot at close range or if a lucky shot from the road got him."

"Maybe Nellie can shed some light on that?"

"Even if she says she did not fire back at the ambushers, I have to keep and open mind. Meaning that, for some reason, she might not be telling the truth. Although I have no idea why that would be."

"Have you had any other trouble in town? Anything recent, that is."

"Several weeks ago, we had a bank holdup. It was kind of strange, in that both the banker and his teller were shot and killed. The two fellows that rode hell for leather out of town right after the hold up turned out not to be the guys that held up the bank. We caught them within ten minutes of the holdup. They were about two miles out of town and watering their horses from the Sweet Water. We rode up to them and they made no effort to get away. We had guns drawn and they were covered by a dozen men. They didn't deny ridin' out of town yelling and raising hell. They claimed they hadn't fired their guns and when I checked them, they hadn't! We brought them in and put them in the calaboose. But, the only two people who could have identified them were dead. The money was gone, but the boys didn't have it. We looked for footprints, but we couldn't find a thing to tie them to the holdup and the killings."

"That is strange," agreed Morgan. "I can't imagine any young cowpuncher riding out of town whooping and yelling without firing his gun! Did you search the route between the bank and the spot where you picked them up? There wasn't some place they could have ditched an extra pair of guns and stashed the bank money?"

"We searched that route over and over. We also looked all around the bank, back alley, everywhere. We just needed one footprint to tie them with the holdup, but we could find nothing! After a couple of days, we had to turn them loose."

"Sounds like they may have been a decoy for the ones who actually did hold up the bank."

Sheriff Locke turned and looked at his riding companion. "Are you a Range Detective, or something? You keep coming up with ideas that I hadn't thought of yet!"

"No," Morgan laughed. "I'm just what you see, a drifter. Bur a mighty curious one."

They rode until they made the turn off for the CR Bar, each man with his own thoughts.

"Couple more things before we actually get to the ranch," advised Wade Morgan. "First, do you know what kind of shot Nellie is with a gun? Either a pistol or a rifle?"

"Well, I've never seen her shoot, if that is what you're asking. But I've heard she is an excellent shot and will at times outshoot the boys! That doesn't go over very well, as you can understand. Now, whether it is pistol or rifle, I don't know!"

"What do her parents think about her showing up the fellows? Surely they know that will cause hard feelings!"

"Well, she doesn't have a mother or maybe she would act more like the girl people think she should be. Now, her Dad just laughs it off. He says he is raising her to take over the CR Bar eventually."

"Uh-huh. Tell me, Jim, has there been anything that you might consider newsworthy happening in Red Rock lately? In the last month or two?"

"Several weeks ago we had a Fourth of July Celebration, but I am unaware of anything that would draw attention to it. There were the usual things, folks shooting off fireworks or more likely their guns. There were some horse races and some shooting contests but nothing in any of those events to create a stir. Picnic in the evening. Then some dancing after the fireworks in the evening. But nothing stands out in my own mind."

"Okay. I just wondered."

A short time later they crested a ridge covered with cedar trees. They pulled their horses to a halt as they looked down into the valley in front of them.

"Now if I were to have a ranch," exclaimed Wade Morgan, "this is what I would want it to look like! Nice ranch house, big barn, several out buildings, well kept corrals and a stream of water wandering along the edge."

"Yup," Locke concurred, "the CR Bar is one of the nicest looking ranches in the area."

"Like I said before, just being curious here: is the place financially stable? I mean, does Charles Robertson make a good living here?"

"As far as I know, but I ain't privy to his personal dealings mind you. I've never heard of him having any money problems. But you never really know."

"Yeah, you don't." Morgan said as they started their mounts down the slope toward the ranch buildings.

The place seemed deserted as they drew up before the house. There were a few chickens scratching around the area and a dog came out to meet them. Then he decided he didn't really know them and went back to his place under the end of the front porch.

"Howdy, Sheriff," came a voice down near the barn. "What brings you out here today?"

They turned to see a lean fellow standing in the doorway of what appeared to be a work shed. He held a piece of harness in his hand. Morgan smiled at the sight.

"Is Chuck or his daughter around?" asked Locke. "Got a few questions I'd like to ask them."

"Not right around the place here," the man replied. "Nellie rode out fairly early this morning. Think she was headed up toward the breaks. Lookin' for strays, I think. Told her she didn't have to do that, that I could go up later, but that young woman is very set on running this ranch when the time comes."

"Are you the foreman here?" asked Morgan.

"Yeah," the man grinned. "I'm Whop Dunbar. Started workin' here when I was about fifteen. Worked my way up to ramrod."

"Whop, this gent is Wade Morgan. He's just a drifter, but he's been helping me out a bit."

"You're the guy that stopped Nellie's team last night, aren't you?" Dunbar recognized the name immediately. "We sure thank you for steppin' in like you did!"

"My pleasure," Morgan smiled.

"Whop, we kind of wanted to ask Nellie some questions. Or maybe her Dad. Hell, both of them if they were around!"

"I'm not sure where Chuck went," the foreman admitted. "And I don't have a notion when Nellie might be gettin' back!"

"What did you think of those reins?" asked Morgan stepping down from Midnight.

"They was cut alright," the foreman declared. "So were the ones on the other side. They just weren't cut enough to break!"

"I'd like to look at them, if you don't mind?" Morgan requested.

"Right in here," Dunbar said, turning back to the inside of the shed. "I haven't touched them yet. Figured I'd get to the broken ones first."

Wade Morgan and Sheriff Locke both looked at the second set of reins.

"My opinion is, they were cut by two different men," Morgan theorized. "One just didn't cut his deep enough to get them to break when Nellie pulled on them."

Whop had a surprised look on his face. "Bet you're right about that! Never thought of it myself."

"What about that horse with the graze across his rump?" continued the drifter. "He didn't want me touching it last night, so I didn't, but I'm pretty sure it was from one of the bullets that were fired at Nellie."

"Yeah, you were right again, mister. I got him in a stall and fastened down so I could look at it and get some stuff on it last night. It was pretty raw and I was glad I had him tied down when I put some disinfectant on him. That stuff burns like blazes on a fresh wound. Then I covered it with some salve to keep the bugs and stuff from gettin' into it. Turned Red out in the pasture cause we aren't going to use him until that gash is healed up. But I could go bring him in, if you wanted to see that bullet burn."

"No, that's okay," said Sheriff Locke. "Both you and Morgan have seen it and I'm sure you both know what you were looking at."

"Whereabouts are those breaks you said Nellie was going?" Morgan continued to pry.

"They are northwest of the ranch here. About ten miles, I suppose, but it is so difficult to get there it is more like you were ridin' fifteen to twenty."

"By the time we could get there it would be getting late and it would put us back to town long after dark," explained the sheriff.

"Maybe we could just ride that way for a spell and could be we'd run onto Nellie coming back," Morgan proposed.

"Yeah, we could do that, I suppose. Any trail or anything leading up there?" he asked the foreman.

"Nope. We don't go up there much. Those breaks would be called 'badlands' by some folks," Dunbar added. "It is a pretty rugged and desolate spot. Chuck don't like them referred to as 'badlands' cause he thinks it gives the ranch a bad name. Me, I don't see that it makes any difference."

"Any landmarks so we'd know if we were heading in the right direction?" asked Morgan.

"You bet. When you get up out of the swale here where the ranch buildings are, look off to the northwest. On a ridge, you'll see a tall pine. Then 'way off yonder, if you look real careful, you'll see a butte stickin' up. Looks like somebody pointin' to the sky with his finger. The butte ain't part of the breaks, or badlands, but by the time you get close to it, you'll be able to see them."

"Don't think we're planning on going that far," Locke clarified. "We just thought we might run into Nellie coming back. If we don't see her, we'll turn and start back toward Red Rock. I reckon we'll just head straight in, so we won't be coming by here."

They mounted, waved to Whop, who waved in return, and headed up the slope northwest of the ranch buildings. When they reached the top, they could see the distant evergreen. Very faintly, in the far distance, was a slender pillar of rock reaching skyward.

"Just like Whop said," Locke pointed it out.

"Yep," replied Morgan, "but I had a feeling as he was talking that he really didn't want us going up toward the breaks."

"Uh-huh, maybe you're right. Word is, he is kinda sweet on the girl. And if she came in last night, all thrilled about this strange guy who saved her and her team, that may not have gone over too well. So Whop may have hoped you wouldn't be going out to meet her!"

"Sheriff, I swear there ain't anything between us. But people can think whatever they want."

Whop Dunbar was right about it being a rough ride to get to the breaks. The terrain was rugged and broken with any number of gullies and washes.

Late in the afternoon, Sheriff Locke suggested they turn around and get started back toward Red Rock. "I've got a couple of deputies that kind of look after things when I am gone, but they didn't even know I was leaving today. I didn't figure we'd be gone this long!"

"Alright," Morgan, pulled Midnight to a stop. "Why don't you ride on back. I think I will mosey on over and take a look at those breaks. There may have been another reason why Whop didn't want us to take a look at that area."

"Suit yourself, Morgan. I suppose there might be something to that. And you might just run into Nellie while you're out here."

"Sheriff, if that girl has any sense at all, she is at least halfway back to the ranch by now. Probably already there. Our chances of running onto her are about zero. However, I would still like to take a look at these breaks or badlands. How much area are we talking about?"

"I don't rightly know. Never had any reason to be in there. It would be a really good place for someone to hide out, though. I think I'll just ride on with you a little while longer, if you don't mind."

"Sure, you can come along. I certainly don't mind the company. Let's get to moving. No real point in trying to look around after the sun goes down."

The two riders picked up the pace as they were aware of the lateness of the day. Shadows were getting long when they reached the first outcropping of barren rocks.

"I been thinking," Locke said as they drew up and looked over the area. "I heard one time, years ago, that there had been some kind of settlement started up here in the breaks. It doesn't make any sense, though. What little I heard was that a few fellows tried to get a town started because they had found some kind of ore back in there."

"Ore?" questioned Morgan. "What kind?"

"Don't know that anybody ever said. It would about have to be gold or silver, don't ya think?"

Morgan nodded. "So what happened to the settlement?"

"I think their strike turned out to be more their imagination than anything else. And I was told there was a creek up here, which doesn't make any sense, and that it dried up, leaving the town without any water. That was the final straw."

"Do you have any idea where this place was located? If there is anything going on up here, that would be the place to start looking around."

"Nope,. I don't have a clue."

Ahead of them lay a canyon, with the terrain sloping downward toward it. Shadows were getting longer and the sun sank lower.

"Gonna be dark afore long," the lawman observed.

"Yeah," replied Morgan. "Think I'll ride down into the canyon. Just go a short distance and see what is in there. I've got to think if there was a settlement up here somewhere; it would be close to the edge. Either that, or close to the spot where they thought they'd made a strike."

"I'm with you," the sheriff said and the two men urged their mounts toward the entrance of the canyon.

They rode slowly as Wade Morgan was looking at the ground trying to determine if anyone had been in the area recently. He realized as he rode along that the constant wind moving the sandy soil would make it difficult for any tracks to remain very long. They had just reached the floor of the canyon and were moving among the dry clumps of grass that grew there when Morgan pulled his big black to a halt.

"That looks like..." he said, as he started to dismount. His comment was interrupted by the crack of a rifle and a startled cry from the sheriff. Several more shots were fired in rapid succession.

Immediately, Wade Morgan pulled his Winchester from his rifle boot and dropped to the ground, slapping Midnight on the rump as he did so. The horse leaped and moved quickly away from the area. The sheriff's horse was following him, but the lawman was on the ground clutching his left arm. Blood was rapidly soaking his shirt sleeve.

Morgan rolled over on the ground and sent three shots upward toward the lip of the canyon on the opposite side. There was no return fire.

"How bad are you hit?" he asked the lawman, who was hunkered down behind a clump of bluestem about ten feet away.

"Stings like crazy," was the reply. "And the blood is soaking my sleeve. But I think it is just a deep crease. We can look at it after we get out of here. How many do you think there are out there?"

"I heard two different guns," said Morgan, "so, at least two. Might have been

"How bad are you hit?"

more. And I am real surprised that anybody would be shooting at us. There must be something in there they don't want us to see."

A few minutes passed and there were no more shots. "I think they have either left or they are waiting to see if we will leave." Morgan finally guessed. "Let's start moving back up the slope."

"Are you going to have any trouble catching your horse?" the sheriff asked.

"No, he'll come on my whistle. Let's work our way toward the mouth of the canyon. And kind of keep something between you and the rim, Okay?"

"Okay, but my bay may be a little spooky."

"Most likely he will follow Midnight."

As they worked their way out of the canyon, Sheriff Locke realized that Morgan's big black was following along some distance behind them. And behind him was his bay.

When they came to a large boulder that would protect them from anyone watching from the canyon rim, Morgan had the sheriff sit down while he examined his upper left arm.

"It is rather deep," Morgan reported, "but I think the bleeding is beginning to slow down. We should bind it tightly for the ride back to town. We don't want it to cut off the circulation, but we do want it snug enough that the jostling you take from riding won't let it get started again."

"Yeah," the lawman agreed and Morgan could see the sweat beading up on the man's forehead.

"How are you feeling? You think you can ride?"

"I can make it. But it is beginning to throb a bit."

"Your shirt is ruined, Jim. I'm going to cut your sleeve off and use it to bind the gash." Morgan pulled a knife out of his belt and quickly cut away the shirt sleeve, then cutting it length-wise, he cut two strips to bind the padding in place over the wound.

"There. That ought to do it. You do have a doctor in town, don't you? I didn't see his office, but I wasn't looking for it either."

"He works out of his house," the sheriff explained. "Doctor Reginald Davis. Folks all call him Doc Davis."

Midnight came up and nuzzled Wade Morgan. The sheriff's bay followed not far behind him. Morgan quietly walked over and took the reins of the bay. Then he led the animal over to the seated sheriff.

Jim Locke got to his feet but it was obvious he was somewhat wobbly. Morgan reached out to steady him. Then he helped the wounded sheriff into his saddle.

"Sure you can do this? We're going to hit a pretty good clip going back into town. Otherwise we'll be spending a good portion of the night just getting back."

"I can do it," Locke said in a hoarse voice. "If you see me getting woozy, just tie me in the saddle so I can't fall off. We'll make it, Morgan."

They walked the horses out of the canyon and then Wade Morgan stepped into his stirrup and they pushed their mounts into a gallop. They rode side by side so the dark clad Morgan could keep a close watch on the sheriff.

From the breaks, they angled directly toward Red Rock which would make the ride around fifteen miles in distance. The going was rough as there was no trail to follow and they occasionally found a ravine or gully they had to ride around as it was too steep along the walls to get into and out of again.

Wade Morgan decided it was about midnight when they arrived in Red Rock. Sheriff Locke was still conscious and he gave directions for getting to the doctor's house. It was actually situated off of Main Street and not far from the church.

There was a light still on in the house and the doctor answered the knock immediately.

"Whoa, Sheriff, what happened to you?"

"He got shot in the upper arm," Wade Morgan supplied.

"And who are you, mister?"

"I'm the fellow who was with him about fifteen miles out of town and helped him get back to Red Rock."

"Alright, glad you were there," the old doctor replied. "Looks like you did a good job binding up the wound. I'll get it opened up and disinfected. Stitches, if need be."

"I don't know Sheriff Locke all that well, doc. Does he have a family, wife maybe, someone to notify?"

"No, there is just him. Lives alone, however, and I want him right here through the night. I will redress the wound in the morning and see how it looks then."

Morgan thought it was a good idea.

"You got a place to stay?" Doc Davis asked a moment later.

"Yeah, I've got a room over at the Starlight. My name's Wade Morgan, in case you need to get hold of me for anything."

"I'm going to give him some stuff to ease the pain and it will likely make him go to sleep. You might check in at his office and see if either one of his deputies might be there. Just let them know where their boss is."

"I'll do that." Morgan started for the door.

"Oh, one other person that will very likely want to know about this would be the little gal that works right across the street from his office. Her name is Becky. I'm not right sure what her last name is, but just ask around. Someone will be able to tell you."

"Johnson," came the raspy voice from the couch where Sheriff Locke was stretched out. "Becky Johnson."

"I'll let her know," Morgan told the sheriff. "Promise."

Wade Morgan went to the sheriff's office where he found a middle aged fellow who identified himself as Slim Cody. He was indeed a deputy and Morgan filled him in on the activities of the evening telling him where his boss was and that he was most likely the man in charge until the sheriff was back on his feet. The man tugged on his chin.

"Like for you to take care of Jim's horse," Morgan added. "It has been ridden pretty hard today."

"Yeah, I can do that," the deputy agreed.

"Good. Now, could you tell me where to find a girl named Becky?"

Slim snickered slightly. "You might try the Golden Nugget. That's where she works."

"You said that, like there is something I should know! What is it?"

"Oh, you're thinkin' she is one of them floozies that takes care of men, but that ain't so. She works back in the kitchen. Likely washing dishes right now, unless she has finished up and gone home."

"Sounds like a girl that has her head on straight!" Morgan said pointedly. "We need more of that kind, both men and women!"

"Yeah, you're right. Sorry if I gave yah the wrong impression and thanks for what yah done for the sheriff."

Morgan tipped his sombrero and exited the office. Back on the street, he crossed over to the Golden Nugget. It was late and there was not much activity anywhere other than the two saloons, and his stomach told him he wouldn't mind sitting down to a good meal. He could do that and, hopefully, talk to Becky Johnson at the same time. He wondered just what her connection was with Sheriff Locke.

Morgan pushed open the batwing doors and walked into the smoky interior of the saloon. He saw the bar running along the side of the room and walked in that direction.

"What'll you have, stranger?" asked the barkeep.

"I'd really like to sit down to some grub, if the kitchen is still open?"

"It's still open. We don't shut down the kitchen until about thirty minutes before we close. Just go right through that open doorway there," the man said, pointing out the way. "There is a small dining area there. Find a table and sit down. Someone will be right with you."

"Thanks." Morgan turned toward the doorway. Then he stopped and looked back. "Is Becky Johnson still around? I've got a message for her."

"Wouldn't be from the sheriff, would it?" the barkeeper asked. "I think she is a little worried cause he was supposed to come by earlier."

Morgan just smiled and turned back toward the dining area. The room was empty so he picked a table not far from the kitchen and sat down. Shortly, the Dutch door swung open and a girl came out. He assumed she was Becky Johnson.

She was on the short side, had freckles and a honey brown color to her hair, which was done in pigtails giving her a little girl look. She was drying her hands on her apron and smiling.

"What would you like, mister?"

"Whatever you've got that is already cooked. I really don't want to wait too long. And some coffee, if it's hot."

"Coffee coming right out and then the grub." She hurried back into the kitchen. She reappeared in just seconds with a pot of coffee and a cup which she placed on the table beside Morgan. She whirled and retreated into the kitchen and a moment later was back with a plate heaped up with meatloaf, potatoes, gravy and green beans. Another plate held four slices of bread.

"This look okay?"

"It looks great. Thank, you Ma'am."

"Good, just call if you need anything else."

"There is one thing." He looked up from pouring hot black coffee into his cup. "Would you happen to be Miss Becky Johnson?"

"Yes. I'm Becky Johnson. Why you asking?"

"Do you have time to sit down for a minute? I have a message for you," Morgan said with his best smile not wanting to spook the girl.

The waitress pulled out a chair and sat down at the table and her face looked much paler. Morgan hoped she was not going to go to pieces when she heard that Locke had been shot.

"Are you pretty close to Sheriff Locke?"

"Yes!" the girl exclaimed. "Why? What's happened? Has Jim been hurt or something?"

"Relax, Miss Johnson. He got a flesh wound and is at Doc Davis's right now. He's okay. Doc just wants him to rest up there. Anyway, Jim asked me to stop by here and tell you." There was immediate relief in the girl's face.

"You're sure it ain't bad?"

"Doc said so. Really."

"Oh, good. I've been waiting for him to come in, as I have some news for him, too. Are you a friend of his?"

Morgan nodded.

"Are you the Masked Rider?" she asked.

Wade Morgan was stunned. "What makes you ask that?"

"Because..." and the girl looked around to see that no one was in the room that would overhear her. Then she leaned closer across the table and whispered to the stranger.

"Because Sheriff Locke knows a man, who says he knows the Masked Rider. Everyone thinks the Masked Rider is an outlaw, but this fellow says he's an outlaw hunter. Jim has asked this friend of his to get in contact with the Masked Rider to see if he would come to Red Rock and help him find the killers who shot up the bank and took all that money."

Becky stopped to catch her breath and saw the stunned look on Morgan's face.

"Oh," she said, her hand going to her mouth, "I guess you aren't. I'm sorry, Mister..."

"Just call me Wade," the stranger said. "Now, Miss Johnson, I have been helping Sheriff Locke because I found a dead body when I came into town earlier. I rode out with him to do some checking on some ideas we had. While we were out on the plains, near the breaks, someone took a few shots at us. One of the slugs caught Jim in the arm. He lost some blood but we got him bound up and back into Doc Davis's place. The doctor gave him something for the pain and it should have put him to sleep by now. He'll be there until tomorrow. He probably had some stitches, but everything should be okay."

"I should go over there right away!" the girl exclaimed, getting up and taking her apron off.

"No. Please, Miss Johnson, all you would do is bother the doctor. Jim is surely asleep by now. When you get off work, you should go home and sleep until tomorrow morning. Then stop by and see him."

"Hmm, maybe you're right. I wasn't thinking," and she put the apron on again.

"Sit down," Morgan offered, "and tell me what you know about this Masked Rider situation. Jim never mentioned it to me. But then I am a stranger and he's known me for less than a day. He did ask me earlier, if I was a Range Detective, so he must have been thinking something along those lines."

"Well, I didn't know he had sent for the Masked Rider, although we did talk about it briefly. But one of my friends came in today and casually mentioned that he thought the Masked Rider had been seen in the area. I don't know just where he was seen, but I thought I should pass that on to Jim. If nothing else, it might take some of the stress off his mind."

"Yeah," Morgan began eating. "I know he is really concerned about that bank robbery and the lack of any evidence. Then, of course, the dead body this morning. And now he has taken a bullet in the arm."

"Well, thanks for letting me know, Mister Morgan." Becky Johnson excused herself and returned to the kitchen. Wade Morgan ate a satisfying meal, placed money on the table and rose to leave the Golden Nugget.

As he passed through the saloon, he saw two men that had not been there earlier. Both were lean and hard looking fellows, though Wade Morgan felt neither of them was much beyond twenty years of age. Each man was carrying two six-guns strapped down. He was sure these were the two gun-slicks the clerk at the hotel had mentioned.

The two fellows were at the bar, each with a glass of whiskey in his hand. Morgan attempted to just walk on by them, but one man happened to see him in the mirror covering the length of the wall behind the bar.

"Hey," the fellow said, turning quickly, "ain't you that new fellow in town we've heard about?" The fellow was loud so that the few customers in the room all heard him.

"Wouldn't know," Morgan replied attempting to step around the man.

"Whoa! Wait up there! I'm talkin' to you!"

"You a gunman?" asked the second fellow.

The Wade Morgan compressed his lips slightly and stopped. "You fellows have asked me two questions. Both of which are no concern of yours! However, I am new in town. I do not consider myself a gunman!" He started to step around the two fellows but they moved to block his way.

"If you ain't no gunman," hissed one of the men, "then what are you doin' wearing two guns tied down?"

"I use 'em to shoot rattlesnakes and coyotes is all."

"Then, if that's all ya use 'em fer, then me and Butch, here, ought to just take 'em off of ya!"

There was a scraping sound on the bar and both rowdies glanced in that direction. They found themselves looking down the double barrels of a shotgun held by the barkeeper.

"Not in my place, boys!" the barkeep snapped. "Either one of you fellows draw your iron, it'll be last thing either one of you ever do! This greener will cut you both in two!"

"Aw, hey, now, Jack," the nearest of the two held up his arms away from his guns, "we was just joshing this fellow! We didn't mean nothin'!"

"Finish your drinks and get out that door!" Jack snapped. "I'm giving you twenty seconds and I count kind of fast!"

Butch and his unnamed partner grabbed their drinks and gulped them down. Then they headed for the door, moving quickly. They were definitely gone in twenty seconds.

"Thanks, Jack," said Wade Morgan. "I'm much obliged!"

"You're welcome, stranger. I've seen you with Sheriff Locke, so I figure you're okay!"

"My name's Morgan, Wade Morgan. What can you tell me about those two?"

"Not much," replied saloon owner. "Call themsevles Butch and Hammer. I don't know where they are from or what they do, but they have been around here for a few weeks. They think they are gun-slingers, but as far as I know, they haven't been able to get anyone to take them on!"

"Interesting. Thanks for the information."

"Did I hear one of them say that Sheriff Locke had been shot. Do you know anything about that?"

"Normally I wouldn't reply to a question like that, but you very likely just saved my bacon, so here is what I can tell you. The Sheriff did a take a bullet in the arm earlier this evening. Don't have any idea who was doing the shooting. However, the Sheriff is over with Doc Davis. He's been patched up and will likely be doing his rounds come tomorrow. I'll let him add whatever he wants to this story."

Jack nodded and Morgan left the saloon.

He stepped just outside the doorway, moved to one side and took a deep breath of fresh air while discretely looking up and down the street. In doing so, he noticed Sheriff Locke's horse was still tied to the rail beside Midnight. The light in the sheriff's office was out, so the deputy had most likely gone home.

Stepping off the board walk, Morgan moved toward the two horses, intending to take them to the North End Livery. He was half way across the street when he heard a sound that caused him to whirl and jump to one side. Coming toward him were the two men from the saloon. Morgan moved again, getting himself so that he was not lined up with the horses.

He filled his hands his six-guns and aimed them dead center at the two approaching men.

Butch and Hammer had been walking toward Morgan with their hands dangling very close to the butts of their pistols. Then, suddenly, they were facing two drawn guns. Quickly they spread their arms away from their weapons and came to a stop.

"You fellows are just asking for an accident," Morgan drawled softly. "So far, you've survived two! The third time might not be so lucky for you! What is it you boys want?"

"Uh," stuttered Hammer, "we just wanted to ask ya a question, mister."

"What would that be?"

"We saw ya bringin' in the Sheriff a while ago and it looked like he had been hurt, maybe shot, or somethin'."

"So?" Morgan was going to tell them anything.

"So...was he shot or something?" pestered Butch.

"I didn't say he got shot," Morgan said. "You said that. He can tell you whatever he wants you to know come tomorrow."

Butch and Hammer looked at each other.

"Don't even think about it, boys, With one hand, very slowly unbuckle your gun belts and let them drop in the street. Then step away from your guns. Do it all slowly and careful like."

Both men began to slowly unbuckle their gun belts. When all four belts and holsters were in the dust, Morgan went over and picked them up. He carried them over to the Sheriff's Office where he placed them in the shadows just around the corner.

"When the sheriff is well, you boys can come and get your weapons. Right now you are coming with me."

"Where we goin'?"

"We are going out to the edge of town, where I am going to show you why you don't want to get in a shootout with me. And if you've got a hideout gun on your person right now, do not make any move that looks like you are trying to get it out! You'll be dead without a second chance!"

Butch and Hammer led the way north up the street while Wade walked behind them leading Midnight and the sheriff's horse. When they reached the North End Livery, he opened the gate to the pasture. He motioned the two men to stand where he could see them as he unsaddled the two mounts. He placed the trappings on a rail in the pasture fence.

"Okay, boys, let's get a little farther out of town. And right over there, Butch, is a gourd vine. Pick two gourds about the size of your fist or a little bigger."

"What for?" growled Butch.

"So that I don't see a need to just shoot you right here!"

Butch quickly gathered up two of the gourds.

They were a couple of hundred yards out of town when Morgan came to a stop and pointed. "Those two fence posts right there, the ones about a yard apart. Place one gourd on the top of each post!"

Butch hurried to do as he was told.

"Now," said Morgan, "I do not claim to be a gunman. That does not mean that I cannot draw quickly and shoot accurately. We are about twenty paces from those posts. Stand right over there where you can see me and the gourds."

When Butch and Hammer were in place, there was a sudden blur and two six-guns barked as one. Both gourds splattered into many small pieces.

Wade Morgan whirled toward the two men, his two guns pointed right at their faces. Both men looked stunned as they stopped fumbling in their clothing trying to get out a weapon while the stranger was busy with his demonstration. Their hands went up.

"I could shoot you both dead right here, right now! Seeing as how you were trying to draw on me!"

The faces of Butch and Hammer blanched white in the moonlight.

"Let me see what you were trying to pull on me," Morgan ordered. "Do it nice and easy. If you make a quick move, you could be very dead!"

Very slowly the two men removed a knife and a small hand gun. Morgan held out his hand and took them both.

"At this point, I planned to letting you go, but there has been a slight change of plans. Get out of your clothes right now! Boots, pants, everything! I need to see what else you've got hidden away."

Amid much grumbling and threats, the two men were soon standing naked in the moonlight.

"Okay, boys, put everything in a pile right here!"

Butch and Hammer soon had their clothing in a pile. The tall stranger reached into his shirt pocket and brought out a match, which he struck. In a moment the stack of clothing was burning brightly.

"You can't do this!" pleaded Butch. "It's against the law!"

Wade Morgan just laughed.

"Fellows, there might be a little bit of wear left in those boots, but I doubt it. The story will be all over Red Rock tomorrow, so if anyone in town comes up missing clothing, they'll know who to blame. If I were you, I'd try to get to a nearby ranch, sometime before morning. The boys in the bunk house might take pity on you and loan you some clothes. And it might be a smart thing for you to stay out of town as long as I am here!"

Mouthing silent threats, the two men started down the road. Morgan assumed they had a place in mind where they would go. It was a cinch their clothing was worthless.

Wade Morgan had just turned toward Red rock, when Blue Hawk stepped out of the shadows.

"*Amigo*, you have much fun this night!"

"Well, if that is what you want to call fun," Morgan chuckeld.

"Looked like fun to me!"

When they reached the North End Livery, they took the saddles from the pasture fence and placed them in the barn. Morgan picked up a small hammer from the work bench inside the door and the two men walked back to the sheriff's office.

"I expect those two fellows will eventually be back for these guns," said Wade

Morgan. "I told them I'd leave them here for them. But I didn't say they'd be in working order."

The two men unloaded all four guns. Then they placed them on a rock and with the hammer smashed the cylinder of each pistol. For good measure, they bent the barrel of each gun.

"*Ammigo*," said Blue Hawk, "do you think those men would walk all the way to a ranch to get clothes and horses when they could steal them right here in town?"

"No, I wouldn't, if I were in their place. I would image they are just about back in the North End Livery right now! Let's go see!"

There were two things Wade Morgan and Blue Hawk often did. One was practice with their guns when they were away from civilization. The other was to do some running. Both men felt that, in their line of work, being able to run could save their lives. And it had many times.

They turned and broke into a steady lope for the livery barn. Breathing deeply, they approached the stable. Morgan carried the small hammer he had borrowed earlier.

"Very quiet," the Yaqui whispered.

"Yeah," replied Morgan, softly. "It is too soon for them to have found clothing and saddled two horses."

"Ah, I hear, something inside barn," the Yaqui pointed ahead.

Wade Morgan stood on one side of the open doorway while Blue Hawk took up a position on the opposite side. In moments they could hear the sound of hooves approaching the door.

When the first man appeared, leading a horse, Morgan reached out of the shadows and tapped him on the skull with the hammer. He went down without a sound.

"Butch, what's wrong?" asked Hammer when he realized his partner was curled up on the ground.

"Him sleep," replied a guttural voice as the point of a knife poked his bare buttocks.

Hammer let out a blood-curdling shriek and then the hard handle of the knife came down on his uncovered head. He folded up with his partner.

The door slammed on the house across the street and the old hostler, Clem, came hurrying across the street carrying a shotgun. With the advent of the hostler, Blue Hawk faded back into the shadows of the barn.

"It's me, Clem! Wade Morgan," he called out, the hammer in his hand.

"Oh, well, howdy, Wade," the old stable man grinned. "I saw you put a couple of horses in the corral and then later Juanita heard a shot. Seemed like it was down the road a piece."

"Yeah. That was me. I was having a problem with a couple of would-be

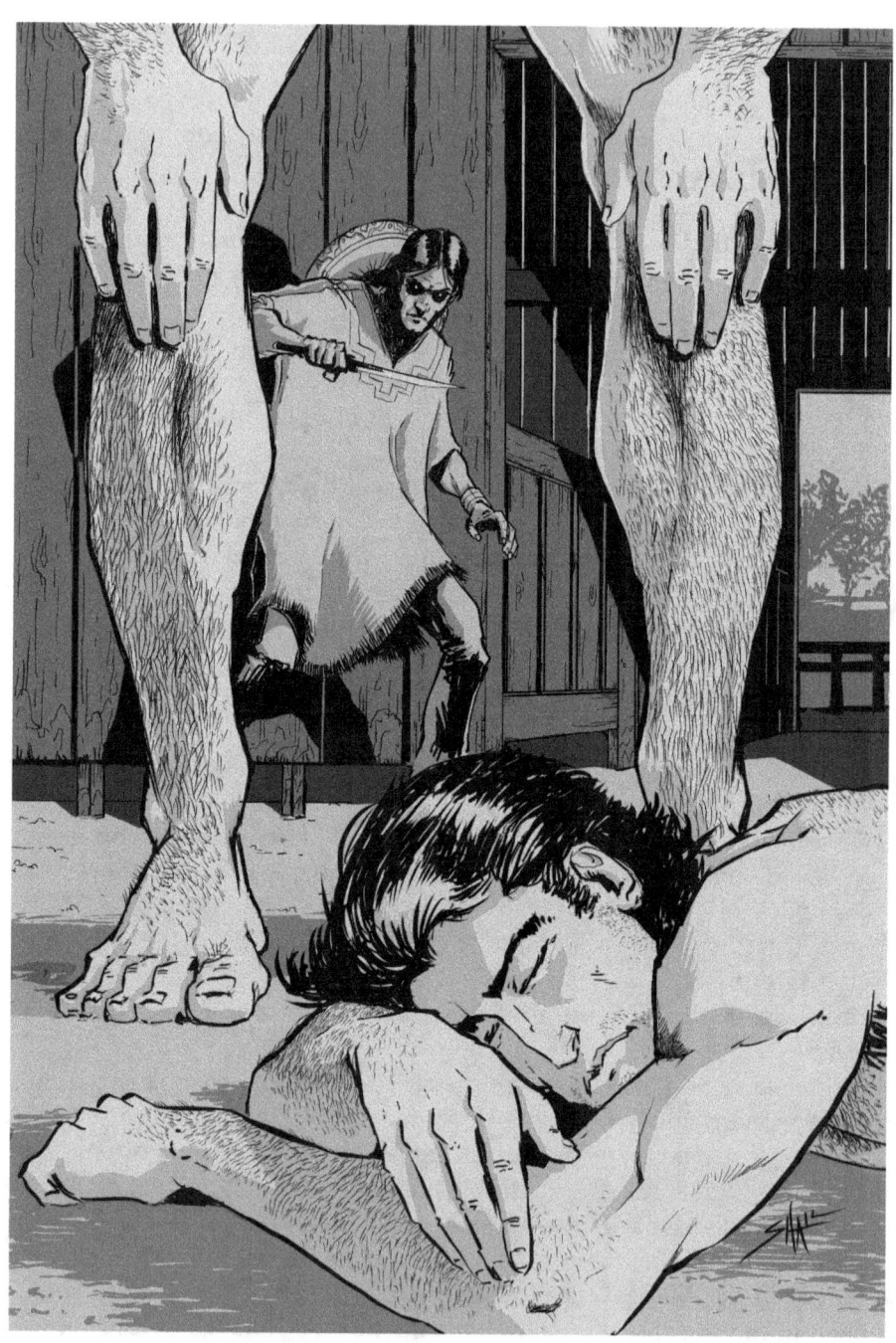

"Butch, what's wrong?"

gunslingers. I thought I had that taken care of, but here they are! Came back to steal a couple of horses!"

"Looks to me like somethin' happened to their duds along the way!" the man cackled as he watched the two men beginning to stir on the ground.

"Yeah, theirs got burned up. I hadn't thought about the problem I might be causing other people when these fellows began trying to steal more clothes. You happen to have some extra stuff they could wear? I'll pay you for it."

"Let me check with Juanita," Clem said. "I'll be right back."

Butch and Hammer were both groaning as they tried to get to their feet. Both men were staggering.

"You fellows seem a little dizzy," observed Wade Morgan. "I'll always heard cold water will help that," and he led them over to the horse tank by the corral. Before either of the two men knew what was happening, they were floundering in the horse tank.

There was laughter and Morgan turned to see Clem walking toward him. "Funniest thing I have seen in quite a while," he said, grinning. "Juanita will bring some old clothes out in a few minutes! She's been watching from the house and she recognized both of these fellows as being gunmen."

Both Butch and Hammer were soaking wet when they finally got hold of the edge of the tank so they could stand up. They stood panting for a few moments and then began to climb out of the tank.

Juanita, a dark middle aged woman, walked up carrying two pairs of overalls and two shirts. Then she began to laugh at the sight in front of her.

"Naked as two new-born babies," she giggled. "Not nearly as cute, though."

"And not any smarter," added Clem.

"Here," said the woman, tossing each man a shirt. "Dry off with the shirt. Then put it on and here are the overalls. You can adjust the straps to make them fit! I sure don't see how come somebody didn't just shoot the two of you! Save the rest of the world a lot of trouble!"

"Do you fellows have horses somewhere?" asked Morgan.

"Down in front of the Golden Nugget," Butch mumbled.

"And, yet, you were trying to steal my horses!" exploded Clem. "I gotta rope in the barn! We'd ought to hang both of ya, right now!"

"But we were naked," cried Hammer, as he pulled on the overalls. "We couldn't go down there lookin' like that! Somebody mighta seen us!"

"Somebody has seen you now!" laughed Juanita. "You're going to be the laughing stock of the town!"

"Was I you," growled Clem, "I'd go down there, get my horses and ride out of town! And never come back!"

"Good advice," Morgan concurred.

"That's what we're gonna do," grumbled Butch.

The two gunmen walked away from the small group at the North End Livery making their way toward the center of Red Rock where their horses were tethered. Their gun belts were also in the shadows of the sheriff's office. They walked carefully as they were barefooted and their feet were tender as they were rarely without the protection of boots.

With the hour being late, Clem and Juanita turned back toward the house across the road from the livery barn.

"Here," said Wade Morgan, holding out a couple of coins, "this ought to cover the cost of their clothing."

"Whoa, that's too much," the old man protested. "They was purt nearly worn out anyhow!"

"But when you go to replace them, you'll be expected to pay full price. Take the coins. Make me happy."

Clem laughed as he took the offered money and slipped into his pocket. "Well, if you insist."

"I'm going to stick around the stable here for a little while," Morgan continued "just in case those two hombres decide to come back this way. I could see them trying to steal something or start a fire just to be mean."

"Want me to stay out here with you?"

"No, I won't be here long. Just enough to make sure they ride on. See you later," Morgan waved walking toward the dark barn.

He was joined by Blue Hawk in the dark interior of the building.

"They are coming this way," said the Indian a few minutes later.

"We'll just stay in the shadows and make sure they ride on by."

Presently Butch and Hammer rode past the livery. They did not stop or even slow down as they rode out of town. Both were hatless and barefooted. However they each had their gun belts around their waists and tied down.

"I'll bet, they never checked the guns before they put them on! Boy, are they in for a surprise!" Morgan chuckled.

Then he and Blue Hawk sat in the darkness of the livery barn and discussed the happenings of the day. They decided that with sunup they would ride out to the breaks and take a look around the ghost town that supposedly existed somewhere out there.

Before dawn, Blue Hawk, now dressed in his native garb, rode Pretty Boy through the sleeping town of Red Rock. Trailing along behind him was the sorrel, Slow Joe. They passed the North End Livery and followed the road out of town, using the same route as the chastised gunmen.

A short distance out of town, the Masked Rider, wearing his mask and *mantilla*, rode out of the trees and joined his Yaqui friend. He raised his hand in greeting and the Indian repeated the gesture. They continued riding in silence.

They did not follow the trail leading out of Red Rock long before they turned off and angled toward the breaks some fifteen miles distance. They had decided the previous evening to take a different route to the area, with the thought that perhaps they could arrive unseen.

They had covered close to five miles when they realized other horses had been over the route recently. It did not seem to be a trail, yet the tracks indicated use at various times. Blue Hawk dismounted and got down on the ground where he could examine the hoof prints more closely.

"Tracks here are those of the two men from last night," he said looking up at the still mounted masked man. "Perhaps they go to the badlands, too. Other prints are too old to tell much. Not made by same horses."

"If Butch and Hammer rode this way," mused the Masked Rider, "then we shall be on the watch for them. It would be possible for them to have shot at the sheriff last evening and still be in town around midnight. Locke and I rode much slower with his injury."

"It was dark when you and the sheriff came into town," recalled Blue Hawk, standing up, "and it would be somewhat difficult to see that the sheriff was actually injured. Perhaps they were aware of the injury because they were there when it took place."

"That's possible, amigo. They also might have seen me taking Jim Locke to the doctor's house. But I doubt they were just sitting around watching people ride by. They would have been in a saloon somewhere."

Blue Hawk and the Masked Rider continued on toward the breaks. But now they rode more carefully, utilizing cover whenever it was available.

When they arrived near the badlands, they set up a camp in a secluded grove of trees in a swale. Slow Joe was unloaded, picketed to graze and the supplies hidden. Then the two men mounted and rode toward the declivity where the shots had been fired at Morgan and the sheriff.

They approached slowly, observing everything as they moved. They did not descend into the canyon but moved along the top rim on the side where the shots had been taken. It did not take Blue Hawk long to locate the spot. The Yaqui was of the opinion there had been only two shooters.

"Let us back track and see if they will lead us to the ghost town here in the breaks," suggested the Indian.

"Alright, Blue Hawk. This is the best lead we've had in locating that old town."

Silently, they followed the footprints through the blowing sand. They went down into a canyon and up the following side where the tracks followed along the edge. They stopped often to listen and to look for anything out of the ordinary. On one such stop, Blue Hawk raised his hand slightly signaling that he had seen or heard something.

"I think I heard a groan," he whispered. "Listen."

For a moment, all was silent and then came a faint sound on the ever-shifting breeze. The Indian motioned and began moving alone the ridge. Soon they came to a narrow trail leading down the slope of the canyon wall. Blue Hawk looked down the pathway and nodded with his head. He moved his Winchester so that it was ready for instant use. The trail curved around the canyon wall and then they came to a wide spot where some vegetation was attempting to grow. The area widened to approximately twenty yards.

"There," the Yaqui pointed with his rifle.

The Masked Rider could see what appeared to be a huddled form in the shadow of a rock. He and his companion spread apart and approached the figure.

The man was groaning intermittently and his face and hands were covered with blood. His shirt appeared to be soaked. His hat, just a short distance away, had several holes in it.

"That's Whop Dunbar," the Masked Rider told Blue Hawk. "He's is the foreman on the CR Bar. Looks like he has been hit pretty hard."

They approached the downed man. He was delirious and only semi-conscious. "Help me!" he said in a raspy voice so low and scratchy that the Masked Rider had difficulty in hearing him. "They got the boss and the girl! Help them!"

The masked man began checking the man's head for wounds and immediately found a crease across his skull that had bled profusely. He soon found another wound on the left shoulder. Those were the only two he found.

"He's lost a lot of blood and that head wound could be a bad one," Masked Rider informed Blue Hawk.

"We need water," replied the Yaqui. "It best we move him now. Take him back to Slow Joe. Maybe he can talk when we get him cleaned up."

The Masked Rider picked up the semi-conscious man and, with Blue Hawk leading the way, they carried him all the way back where Midnight and Pretty Boy waited. They sat him on a saddle and, holding him in place, they were soon in the swale where Slow Joe was grazing.

Blue Hawk propped him up against a rock and began cleaning his face and wounds. The cool water began to bring Whop around and his eyes seemed to lose their glazed look. They gave him a drink from the canteen and that, too, helped to revive him.

"Hey, you're masked!" he exclaimed in a hoarse voice. "Are you an outlaw? Are you with those skunks here in the breaks?" Then he sank back against the rock, panting with ragged breathing and looking hard at the masked figure helping him.

"No, sir," Masked Rider answered. "We are not the men who attacked you. We're here to help you. Just forget that I wear a mask."

Whop Dunbar accepted the Rider's explanation.

"Can you tell us where this abandoned town is located?" the Masked Rider asked. "We believe that is where the outlaws are holed up."

For several minutes, the wounded foreman told the masked man and Indian how to find the ghost town. He told them his boss and the man's daughter had ridden out to the breaks the previous day and had not returned. He had ridden out to search for them, thinking there had been some kind of accident. When he approached the breaks, he had been shot at and had to take cover. It had been dark and the shooters did not find him. Whop had hidden on the canyon trail and then lost consciousness. He began to regain his senses as the Masked Rider and Blue Hawk carried him out of the breaks.

Dunbar was exhausted from talking and stopped often to catch his breath.

"You remain here," ordered the Masked Rider. "We will leave you water and Blue Hawk found your rifle. Just stay quiet and rest. We will check out the situation in the old town and see what is going on. Eventually we will return and take you in to see Doctor Davis. He needs to take care of your wounds."

The injured man nodded slightly. "Good luck. I hope you can find Nellie and her dad." He stopped speaking, panting from the exertion. He closed his eyes briefly and when he opened them again, the Masked Rider and Blue Hawk were gone.

They rode the short distance back to the breaks where they dismounted and tried to hide their horses among the scrub brush growing nearby. On foot, the pair entered the area of weathered canyons and blowing sand. It took an hour of careful maneuvering, but they were finally at a point where they could look down and the remnants of the old ghost town.

Below the edge of the canyon wall they could see four buildings, three of which did not look inhabitable. The remaining building appeared to have been repaired recently and there was a faint wisp of smoke spiraling up from the chimney.

A short distance from the cabin was a corral containing several horses. Surprisingly, there was a small stream of water that appeared to be coming from the base of the canyon wall and winding its way along the canyon floor. However, it only covered a little more than a hundred yards before it disappeared into the sandy floor. The occupants had dug a pool to hold the water and enclosed it within the corral, giving their mounts access to it.

"Those are the two horses Butch and Hammer were riding," said Blue Hawk.

"There are three CR Bar horses in there," added the Masked Rider, "plus another eight. If every man has two horses that is at least four!"

"More than four," Blue Hawk corrected. "If one or two men are out keeping a watch for anyone riding in, they surely rode out. They would not walk."

The Masked Rider scratched his chin. "Those three CR Bar horses…surely that would represent Whop, Nellie and her dad, Charles Robertson. We found Whop, so where is the girl and her father?"

"Inside the cabin, maybe," Blue Hawk surmised.

"It still bothers me, Blue Hawk. They tried to kill Whop. They shot at the sheriff and wounded him. Do they actually want anyone alive? Nellie and her father may already be dead out there somewhere."

Blue Hawk merely nodded.

"I'd like to know who or what is in that cabin," the Masked Rider said. "We can get down the side here and if we keep those older cabins between us and the occupied one, we should be able to get rather close. Perhaps we can see or hear something if we are closer."

Ten minutes later, they were on the canyon floor and had worked their way among the fallen down structures and near the one occupied building.

"Watch the front door," said the masked man to his companion, "and I will slip around to the back side and see if I can hear anything."

"Want me to shoot anyone who comes out?"

The black clad Rider shook his head negatively. "Only if they are shooting at you. There may be too many of them in there for us to take on by ourselves. We may need to get some help from Red Rock and Sheriff Locke."

A few minutes later, the Masked Rider lay flat on the ground at the back side of the cabin. He could hear indistinct voices from within the building, but he could not make out what they were saying. What disturbed him was that he was sure he had heard two distinctly feminine voices. One would have been expected as that could be Nellie. But two?

At that moment, a rifle shot sounded loud and clear. Then there were two more shots that sounded as though they were farther away.

The Masked Rider wondered if they were loud enough for the inhabitants of the cabin to have heard them. He listened carefully. All the talking within the building had ceased.

Finally a voice said, "Check that out, Hammer! See what's going on out there!"

Quietly, the masked man rose to a kneeling position, his Winchester held ready. The front door of the cabin opened and closed. He could hear someone saddling a horse at the corral and he knew that Hammer would soon be riding out to check the spot where they had a sentinel set up.

Carefully the Masked Rider worked his way back to the dilapidated cabin where he had left Blue Hawk. His friend was not there.

"Up here." The Masked Rider looked up to see his partner positioned on a few beams that had formed the loft of the cabin.

"There are several people in the cabin," the Masked Rider mouthed softly. "Two women. Several men. I am going in the front door. They will not expect me and I should be able to get the drop on them. Give me a few seconds and then you come in. Be careful who you shoot!"

The Masked Rider stepped out of the run down cabin and walked calmly toward the building containing the outlaws. He doubted that anyone would see him as the windows had been covered when someone had made the place habitable again.

The Rider propped his Winchester up beside the door. Then he drew a six-gun with his right hand and opened the door with his left. As he stepped into the room, he drew his second gun. He immediately moved away from the door.

"Don't anyone move!" he barked loudly.

Bound tightly in a chair was Charles Robertson. His head sagged forward and his chin was on his chest. He appeared to have been beaten and was unconscious. Tied in a chair beside him was his daughter, Nellie. She was staring wide-eyed at the masked man dressed in black.

Five other individuals were in the room, three of them masked. As one, they whirled to see why Hammer had returned so quickly.

The fellow who seemed to be in charge of the group, clawed for his six-gun. A bullet from the Masked Rider's gun drilled him just to the left of his breast bone. Without a sound, he sank to the floor dead.

"Don't do it!" warned the man in black, but the second unmasked man already had his gun out. He whipped it up and fired. The bullet went over the Masked Rider's shoulder and buried itself in the wall. Then a small black hole appeared in the fellow's forehead and blood began to trickle down his face. He sprawled backwards on the floor.

Blue Hawk was in the doorway when the third outlaw began grabbing for his gun. His Winchester roared knocking the man back on the table.

"Don't try it!" warned the Masked Rider glaring at the remaining two masked members of the group, his six-guns held menacingly. Smoke curled from their barrels.

"Take your masks off!" He commanded them.

Slowly hands reached up and removed the masks. The Masked Rider was quite surprised to see two girls standing before him.

"Remove your guns and place them on the table by the dead man." He motioned with one of his pistols.

The girls carefully did as they were told.

"Untie Nellie and her father. Then remove the dead man's mask."

One of the female outlaws untied Nellie while the other one released the ropes that bound Charles Robertson.

To Morgan's surprise, when Nellie was untied, she stood up and hugged the girl who had untied her. Then Nellie turned and hugged the other girl.

"Am I to treat you as an outlaw, too?" he asked Nellie. He lowered his voice hoping the girl would not recognize him as the man who had stopped her runaway team.

"No, no," she said. "You are the Masked Rider, right? My Dad, here, is the man who sent for you. We are so glad to see you!"

"What about the other two girls?"

"They started out playing like they were outlaws for fun. Then they got in too far and before they knew what to do, these men took over! They've been trying to get away, but it became impossible for them to do so. They are very good friends of mine."

"Keep them away from their guns on the table," cautioned the Masked Rider, still unsure about Nellie had said. He stepped around and lifted the mask of the dead man by the girls' guns.

He was not surprised to see Butch. Then, out of curiosity, he checked the dead man's gun. It was still the mangled piece of metal he and Blue Hawk had left for the outlaws. The man had never checked his guns. The Masked Rider doubted that Hammer had checked his weapons either. And they claimed to be gun slingers!

Charles Robertson was groaning as he got to his feet. "Glad to see you," he said, holding out a bloodied hand. The Masked rider shook it.

"How many more outlaws are there?" Asked the Rider.

"Three," Nellie answered quickly. "That fellow, Hammer, and two guards out there on the cliffs. We heard shots and he went to check. Was that you?"

"No. I don't know who that was, so we had best be prepared. You outlaw girls, drag these bodies outside and away from the cabin. Sheriff Locke can send someone up to get them tomorrow. Nellie, see if you can find some water and clean up your father. He'll feel a lot better when he has been washed up."

Nellie immediately began cleaning her father's face and hands and the transformation was remarkable.

"I feel good now," he said after a few minutes. "Just let me get a gun and I'm ready to face those other two hombres!"

"You just relax," Masked Rider said. "Blue Hawk is out checking on that situation right now and I'm sure it will soon be under control."

The Masked Rider stepped outside where the girls were dragging the body of the first man he had shot. He was a big fellow and then he noticed his feet. They were exceptionally small!

"Girls," he said walking toward them, "which one of you shot that fellow south of town the other night?"

They both straightened up and looked at the Masked Rider in surprise. One of them began to cry softly.

"We didn't do it," said Margaret; the other girl. "Red was Elizabeth's boy friend and he wanted out, too! Big Jack came back and said Nellie had returned fire and got him! Nellie is a very good shot, you know. But when we asked her about shooting Red, she was totally surprised. She said she did not return fire. And we believe her. She wouldn't shoot at something she couldn't see."

"So Big Jack shot him because he wanted out," finished the Masked Rider.

"He was supposed to shoot Nellie to prove he was a real outlaw!" sobbed Elizabeth.

"He couldn't do it, so Big Jack just shot him!" said the first girl.

A bird call floated on the wind and the Masked Rider turned to see Blue Hawk approaching. He was leading two horses. A dead man was draped over one and Whop Dunbar was on the other one.

"Looks like we are down to one unaccounted for," said the masked man.

"No, amigo," said Blue Hawk with a slight smile on his face. "Only two horses, so we leave one dead man behind!"

"I didn't hear another shot."

Blue Hawk patted the knife in his belt.

When all the corpses had been placed side by side outdoors, the Masked Rider, Blue Hawk and their friends gathered inside the cabin. This included Whop Dunbar, who stood beside Nellie, Charles Robertson and the two girl outlaws.

"One thing we have not touched on yet," said the Masked Rider. "Do either of you girls know anything about that bank robbery?"

Both girls nodded affirmatively.

"The money is hidden in the old mine shaft," said Margaret. "I don't think anyone ever touched it, so it should all be there. Elizabeth and I carried it out of the bank about thirty minutes before Big Jack and Claude shot the banker and the teller. They weren't supposed to shoot anybody, but they came back and said they couldn't leave any witnesses!"

"What about the two kids that were originally held as the possible robbers? Were they actually involved?"

"I don't think so," said Margaret. "I think that was just a coincident."

"Are we going to be held for the murder of the bankers?" Elizabeth was scared.

"That is out my hands," replied the Masked Rider. "That's up to Mr. Roberson and Whop. They've both heard your stories and can proceed accordingly. But I have one more question. Nellie, why were you coming back out here to the breaks?"

"Originally, Elizabeth and Margaret got to playing like they were bad guys,"

Nellie began. "They didn't hurt anyone and they didn't steal anything. They wanted me to join in with them because of my ability to shoot a gun. I just wasn't interested, but I did know more about them than anyone else did. I figured it was their group that had shot at me and I came out here to let them know I did not appreciate that! I didn't know there was a gang varmints out here!"

"So why were your reins cut?"

"As I said, they wanted me to join their group, although I didn't know what gang it was. It was Big Jack's way of showing me what kind of trouble I could be in, if I didn't join up with them. I don't know what Big Jack's plans really were. But some of the gunmen he surrounded himself with were real duds!"

At that the Masked Rider chuckled.

"Nellie, you take Blue Hawk and go up to that mine shaft and bring down the bank money. We'll be getting the horses here saddled and ready to ride. Whop and Mr. Roberson look like they could make it all the way back to Red Rock. You fellows are going to make Jim Locke one happy sheriff!"

Nellie Robertson arrived back in camp carrying the saddle bags filled with the loot from the bank holdup. There she met the others but when she looked around, she did not see either Blue Hawk or the Masked Rider.

A short time later the group, led by Charles Roberson and his foreman, rode out of the breaks. Nellie looked back hoping to see some sign of the Masked Rider. There was nothing.

"Dad," she said, "I'm sure glad you sent for the Masked Rider!"

"Nellie, dear, I didn't send for him. Sheriff Locke and I talked about it but the Masked Rider moves about so much, you wouldn't have any idea where to get in touch with him. In many places, he is a wanted outlaw, so he has to make sure no one knows how to find him."

"So you mean it was all just by luck that he showed up when he did?'

Roberson grinned at his lovely daughter. "Best darn luck for us. That's for sure."

At that moment, the Masked Rider and Blue Hawk were miles away, loping along with Slow Joe keeping pace behind them.

THE END

WHY WRITE A MASKED RIDER STORY?

The answer to that question is quite simple. I wrote a Masked Rider story because I couldn't write a Lone Ranger story, plain and simple.

I have always been a fan of the Westerns: movies, TV shows, books, comics, pulps, radio programs and newspaper strips. My favorite has to have been Red Ryder as I could follow him daily in the newspaper comic section. The Lone Ranger was a close second followed by Zorro and the Cisco Kid.

In my basement collection, I have seventy-five of the approximately one hundred pulp issues in the Masked Rider run. No, at this point of the game, I am really not interested in finding the remaining issues.

I came along around the end of the pulp era and purchased only a few of the titles I wanted to read from the magazine racks. It was later, when I had a little more loose change, that I began to pick up back issues from second hand shops and the collection was started. All those very early issues that I purchased were *read to death* by all my brothers and sisters. Most of the comic books and Big Little Books that I purchased suffered the same fate.

In writing the Masked Rider story, I floundered a bit and the editor was kind enough to pull me up from the deep water. And I thank him very much!

It is my earnest hope that you do enjoy this Masked Rider story!

JOHN ROSE—The fellow responsible for this Masked Rider yarn was born and raised in south central Kansas, in the wheat and cattle country. John R. Rose had seven brothers and sisters, all younger and all out there on that sand hills farm. They all attended a two room elementary school and all of them became voracious readers. They lived by the county line and had access to both of the county libraries, of which they made very good use.

He graduated from high school and attended Pratt County Community College, known as a Junior College back then. He finished his degree at Fort Hays State University in Hays, Kansas.

He was active in high school sports, taking part in football, basketball and track & field. He continued with basketball and long distance running during college as it helped pay the cost of obtaining an education.

John R. Rose (1939-2018) Retired as a Kansas public school teacher after 37 years. He spent his retirement writing pulp stories and is survived by his wife Meredith, son Michael, who lives in Colorado, and daughter Anne Marie, a resident of Arizona.

WILD BILL HICKOK

"Wild Duck"

by Alan J. Porter

New Mexico, 1860

Shooting a bear in the head was never going to be a smart move. But to the twenty-three year-old James Butler Hickok it had seemed like a good idea at the time. The reality was that no matter how dumb it may seem in retrospect, he didn't really have much choice at the time.

The day had started like many others for the freight driver. He'd rolled out from under the protection of his battered and road-worn wagon, brushed the dirt and dust from his clothes, washed as well as he could with the brackish water that was still left at the bottom of the barrel lashed to the side of the wagon. A reminder that he needed to find some fresh running water soon. A short breakfast that mainly consisted of coffee, made with the same brackish water, and some smoked buffalo meat jerky, then he hitched the horses and headed off for another day on the trail headed towards Sante Fe. Another day, another dollar. It wasn't the life he'd imagined when he'd left Illinois, but it was a job, and it paid.

While he was good with his guns, few opportunities to use them had presented themselves so far, and the excitement he craved was elusive. Although he had started to make something of a name for himself among the residents of the towns along the trails he traversed, not so much for any brave deeds, or gun play, but for the way he liked to announce his arrival with a flourish, racing in at speed, and swinging the wagons around raising as much dust as he could to send anyone on the street scurrying for cover.

Hickok smiled to himself at the thought of the next town ahead; if he got a move on he may be able to sleep in a real bed this evening. As the wagon crested a slight rise in the road the young driver heard the faint sound of rushing water ahead. Seemed like a local creek might be full. Fresh water, a cooling drink, and a wash loomed large in his imagination. A crack of the reigns goaded the horses into some extra effort, although they neighed their disapproval and reluctance. Hickok ignored it and drove them on. Rounding the next corner the reason for their reluctance soon became apparent.

He'd been right about the creek. It was full of flowing water, the early morning sun glinting off its surface. It was inviting, a perfect place to refresh his supplies, get a drink, and maybe even bathe. Except for one thing.

Settled at the edge of the creek was a large red-brown cinnamon bear, keeping watch on her two cubs as they splashed about in the shallow water by the bank. The sound of the wagon had alerted her to Hickok's presence.

The horses started to buck, and Hickok had no choice other than to pull them to a stop, rather than risk them running off uncontrolled and dragging him and the wagon with them. The mother bear moved up from the creek and stood her ground in the middle of the trail, as if challenging the driver to try and get around her.

Faced with three hundred pounds of immovable ursine muscle, the young Hickok leapt down from the wagon, and ran towards the animal shouting at the top of his voice, believing that it would react and hopefully move off the trail and back towards her cubs. It reacted, but not in the manner he had hoped. It started to move towards him. Still running he drew the pistol from his belt, and fired.

An old gun, bought at some out of the way trading post, along with ammunition of doubtful age and effectiveness, was not what Hickok needed at that point. But that was what he had. The bullet was fast and powerful enough to scratch the bear's hide, but that was about it. The round ricocheted off the animal's skull. If it had been protective and defensive in its posturing before, now it was just plain angry, and that anger turned to action.

The bear charged. Before the young driver knew what was happening he was caught by the strong arm of the bear as it pulled him towards her body and slowly started to crush the breath out of him. His right arm with the gun in hand was pinned between his and the bear's chest, but the left was free. He managed to switch the gun over to his left hand and raised his free arm taking another shot. His aim was wild and the bullet struck the bear's paw. Even more enraged the wounded animal swept his left arm upwards with her wounded paw until she could grab it between her powerful jaws. As she started to bite down Hickok was amazed to realize that her breath smelled faintly of fruit and berries. It was a strange final thing to notice he thought, convinced that he was going to die. So much for glory. So much for his future. He'd die here on some unnamed trail path, snack time for a mamma bear and her cubs. There'd probably not be enough of him left for anyone to bury, that's if anyone missed him in the first place. James Butler Hickok was a nobody, and nobody cared about him.

The acceptance of his fate cleared the young man's mind. Sure he was in pain. He was certain a couple of ribs had been broken, and his left arm was a miasma of torn flesh, mangled muscle, and broken bone. Yet that moment of clarity was enough for him to realize that his attacker was so focused on making a meal of his arm that it had eased up some of the crushing pressure. His right arm was free. Reaching down Hickok found the pommel of the bowie knife tucked in his belt. With his last vestiges of strength he pulled the knife free, and slashed upwards. The blade found its target at the bear's throat. A fountain of blood erupted from the animal and coated the struggling man. He kicked, wriggled, and pulled as the wounded beast staggered. Her jaw went slack and he pulled his damaged arm free, and managed to take a step backward freeing himself from its clutches. The animal made a lurch as if to move towards him. It was met with several more thrusts of the bowie knife. At last the bear fell dead at his feet.

Having escaped his fate as bear food, Hickok wasn't about to die on the trail. He was going to make it so that people remembered his name. The pain from broken bones in his chest, arm, and shoulder was almost beyond comprehension. He'd lost a lot of blood. But he was determined to survive. More by instinct than thought, the young driver dragged his broken body back to the wagon he had so cavalierly leapt from just a few minutes before.

There were no clouds of dust, or wild patterns made in the streets when James Hickok arrived at the next town on the trail. There was just blood. Blood that would nurture the seeds of legend.

"Nebraska! Why the hell are you sending me to Nebraska?"

"Let's face it kid," the official from the Overland Stage Company shifted uncomfortably in his chair. He didn't like to be the one to deliver bad news, "You've been through hell. We're all surprised you're still around, but it's been four months now."

"I got lucky."

"Lucky, doesn't cover it son. But there's no way you can drive again, an' you're still walking funny." The official paused for a few beats before continuing, "That left arm is useless which means you can't be a guard on a wagon train no longer."

"So you sendin' me to middle of nowhere Nebraska?"

"Look kid, be thankful the company is keepin' you on and transferring you to lighter duties. They could just as easily kicked you out."

"Lighter duties - what does that mean?"

"Assistant stock-tender at a place the company just acquired a share in. Rock Creek Station."

Taking care of horses wasn't exactly Hickok's idea of adventure. But it did provide him with a few benefits. In many ways the task acted as a form of physical therapy that helped his battered left arm rebuild its muscle and range of movement. So focused was Hickok on its recovery that he became as dexterous with the once damaged arm as he was with his naturally dominant right.

The work was hard and the young man didn't get much, if any, chance to go into town. So it was that Hickok's hair grew longer with his days out in the yard working the stock. The long hair and his growing muscular frame soon attracted the attention of the ladies who visited the way station. And one in particular seemed to take an extra interest in the young man.

"Sandra Schull," the name sounded delightful to Hickok's ears as the station manager, Horace Wellman, answered the question as to the identity of the stunning beauty who seemed to linger around the corral just a touch longer than was necessary.

"She is a looker." Hickok mumbled semi-audibly, "You reckon she'd take up with a fellah like me?"

"There's only one way to find out." Wellman smiled. "Go ask her."

"I can't do that." Hickok stepped down from the fence rail where he'd been perched watching the object of his affections from afar. "She's too good for me."

"Boy, she's just right for you. She's only a couple of years older than you, and by the way she looks at you, I'm a thinking the attraction is mutual."

With that encouragement still running through his mind, James Butler Hickok strode across the corral in the direction of Miss Sandra Schull, his stride long and purposeful. Until he reached the halfway mark where his resolved faltered. The reason for his sudden uncertainty was the arrival of a new player on the stage. Dave McCanles, the original owner of the way station, strode out of the nearby ranch house, and without asking had hooked his arm around the young lady's waist and guided her away from the corral. As he did so he turned back, and waved at the young Hickok. "Better luck next time Duck Bill."

"You shouldn't let him call you that." Horace Wellman was now stood alongside his dejected young friend.

"He don't mean no harm by it."

"Don't be fooled. He ain't a man to toy with, and he's got a grievance agin the company. They still haven't paid him what they promised for this place." Wellman imparted this information as he patted Hickok on the shoulder, and turned to head back to the rooms at the back of the stables where the two men bunked down. "I could do with a coffee."

"I'll be along in a minute," Hickok called after the station manager. As he watched his boss walk away James Butler Hickok made two vows to himself. One, that he would get to know Miss Sandra Schull a lot better, and two, that he would stay out of the company's business.

One of those vows he would manage to keep, the other would prove to be impossible.

The mid-July heat was oppressive; it was hot enough to stick your shirt to your back just by walking out the door. As the mercury rose so did men's tempers, and their passions too. It was the latter that occupied Hickok's mind, and other parts, as he and Sandra Schull concluded their intimate rendezvous in the hayloft of the Rock Creek Station barn. The two young lovers lay in each other's arms basking in the afterglow of what had become an increasingly regular series of encounters. Sandra leant over, and brushed Hickok's growing locks away from his face. As she gazed down at his features she smiled, "You're getting way too pretty, Bill."

"Ah wish you wouldn't call me that. My given name is James."

"I'm just a teasin' yah."

He scowled at her, breaking the mood, and sat bolt upright. The voice dropped a register as if to underscore his displeasure. "McCanles meant that nickname as an insult, said I had lips that stuck out like a duck's bill."

"That's ridiculous Bi… James. And you knows it. Don't take no heed as to what that man says."

"Well you sure do."

"What do you mean by that?" The loving tone also disappeared out of Sandra's voice. She was hurt and confused.

"I've seen you when he comes around, putting his arms around your waist, patting you on the behind without you objectin'."

"He don't mean nuthin' to me."

Hickok rolled away from the conversation, he didn't like the way it was heading. As he reached for his pants and pulled them on he muttered, "Well perhaps I ought to remind him just whose woman you are."

The horseshoe hit him square in his back. It stung and its impact made him flinch with a moment's pain. He was sure it was going to leave a bruise. "I ain't no-one's woman" Sandra shrieked at him. "You can forget havin' your way with me again, Bill Hickok," she deliberately emphasized the detested nickname, "and another thing. Ah don't mind the smell of honest hard work on a man, but you're startin' to stink. If you wanna keep those pretty looks, you ought to bathe more often." The anger had started to subside and the later comment had been accompanied by a partly suppressed giggle.

Hickok rolled back towards her and drew her towards him. "Look I didn't mean it that way. You're your own woman. I know that." He leant closer towards her, meaning to kiss her. He stopped suddenly.

"Why you stop?" she asked.

"Didn't you hear that?"

"I didn't hear nothin'"

"Horses, several of them."

"Nothin' unusual in that," Sandra pouted, "It is a way station after all."

Hickok felt uneasy, and once more pulled himself away from her arms. This time he crawled over to the hatch in the eaves that covered the hole where the hay was forked out into waiting wagons below. He eased the wooden covering aside and peered down towards the ranch house that was now serving as the station master's home. There were four horses being reigned up outside.

"McCanles." Hickok muttered, "But I don't recognize the others."

"Let me take a look," Sandra pushed Hickok slightly to one side and peered out. "Two of his hangers-on by the look of it. Looks like the two James." She turned and half-smiled at Hickok, "Seems to be a day for the Jameses." Turning back she continued, "Yep it's them, Woods and Gordon."

"Whose the other one?"

"Well what did he bring him for? If he's here I doubt McCanles has come looking for trouble."

"Who?" Hickok asked again.

"The fourth rider is William McCanles. His son. He's only about twelve years old I reckon."

"Old enough to hold and shoot a gun." Hickok remarked ruefully.

"You ain't gonna shoot a kid!" Sandra Schull was horrified.

"I ain't plannin' on shooting anyone." Hickok grabbed his shirt and gun belt, shrugged them on, and slipped his bowie knife into the belt. "I'm just gonna go down there and see what they want with Mr. Wellman is all." When he reached the door of the barn Hickok stopped and checked to see where all the players were. Woods and Gordon, with pistols drawn, were loitering in the front yard. McCanles, with his son alongside him was on the porch by the front door hollering for Wellman to appear. For the first time Hickok noticed that McCanles was carrying a shotgun. He turned and looked back at Sandra. "Change of plan. You stay here" And with that he disappeared back into the barn's interior.

McCanles voice carried across the Rock Creek Station yard like rolling thunder in the still humid air. He was an angry man. "Wellman, get your ass out here. I've a message for those thieving sons of bitches that pay your wages."

Horace Wellman was a company man. Loyal to a point, and that point had been reached. No way was he going to face a mad man with a short temper and a shotgun. Discretion was the better part of valor. He retreated further into the interior of the ranch house. His wife, however, felt somewhat different. She placed her hand on the door handle and started to pull it open. What are you doing woman?" Wellman cried out, "He'll kill you."

"He won't shoot a woman. I'll tell him you're not here. Maybe he'll ride off and calm down some." Before Wellman could stop her, she pulled the door open and stepped outside. To be confronted by the barrel of a shotgun leveled at her face. She ignored it. "Listen here David McCanles, you don't go throwing your weight around here. This ain't your place no more."

"It sure is. Those thieves that put bread on your table missed another payment. So the way I see it, this place is still mine and you all are now trespassin."

"Then your beef is with the Overland Stage Company, not my husband." The sound of a door creaking from inside the ranch house behind her made her momentarily look back. She smiled at something. McCanles took it for a smirk at his expense. An insult to a man already insulted, and from a woman no less. He swung the barrel of the shotgun and smashed it into the side of the woman's face, opening up a gash on her cheek. She staggered back into the house and was caught in the strong arms of the station's assistant stock-tender. He led the bleeding woman to a seat at the kitchen table then stepped forward towards the door.

"What are you doing here, boy" McCanles continued to wave the shotgun around.

"You think you should be wavin' that thing around with your boy stood next to you?" Hickok asked, "Thing might go off and hurt someone."

"I'm aimin' to hurt someone all-right" McCanles responded. "I need to send a message to the Overland Stage that I'm no pushover."

"You need to calm down McCanles."

"Your telling me to calm down. You go struttin' around with that stupid face and flowing locks like some city dandy from back East. You ain't nobody stock boy. And don't think I don't knows what you and that strumpet Sandra Schull have been up to."

Hickok bristled at the mention of Sandra's name and stepped forward. "You need to leave, now. Or this ain't gonna end well."

McCanles stepped back too, and shouted around Hickok towards the ranch house interior. "Come on out Wellman, our quarrel ain't none of the stock boy's business."

"You made it my business by threatening my boss, and insulting my woman."

"I'll talk to him James." Wellman's voice came from inside the house, "See if we can settle this like businessmen."

McCanles pushed past Hickok into the house dragging his son along with him. Hickok followed.

Horace Wellman was sat on the wooden bench that provided seating for those at the kitchen table. He was holding a wet cloth to his wife's injured face, trying to staunch the blood seeping from the wound. The architect of the injury stood a few feet away and continued to berate the couple. The tension in the ranch house grew. McCanles wasn't going to get the answers he wanted from a man who was paying more attention to his wife than to him. McCanles raised the shotgun and pointed it at the distracted Horace Wellman.

From the corner of his eye, McCanles saw "Duck Bill" Hickok raise his right hand. He turned. "I told you, this ain't your fight stock boy."

In James Butler Hickok's right hand a Navy Colt demonstrated that he did in fact consider it his fight after all.

In his hand, a Navy Colt demonstrated that he did consider it his fight.

McCanles was dead before he hit the floor, the bullet from the Navy Colt having pierced his heart. Shocked, the young William McCanles dropped to his father's side and knelt over the body, his face buried in the folds of the dead man's jackets. He was oblivious to what happened around him.

Still loitering outside, James Woods was the first to respond to the noise of the gun fire and headed for the ranch house. As soon as he reached the doorway he also felt the impact of one of Hickok's bullets. The aim this time wasn't as accurate. Woods spun around from the force of the impact, and staggered back out onto the porch. Blood seeped from between his fingers as he clutched his chest. "I'm shot!" he called at his companion, and took a couple of steps towards the porch steps. As he reached the top of the steps, the loss of blood took over and he keeled over falling into a patch of scrub and weeds at the side of the steps.

James Gordon saw his companion stagger out of the house and for a moment considered going to help him. Until he saw the long-haired stock boy follow the wounded Woods out of the door, with the formidable, injured, and angry, Mrs. Wellman not far behind. He turned and ran for cover, but it was too late. The Navy Colt spoke again and Gordon felt like he'd been punched in the back. As he pitched forward he saw the creek that ran through the station property lying tantalizingly a few yards in front of him. Pulling himself up onto his knees and elbows he started to drag himself forward hoping to find cover, all thoughts of helping his companion forgotten with his own drive for survival.

Hickok ignored the fallen figure of Woods lying in the weeds as he headed down the house steps and followed Gordon, who had managed to pull himself to his feet and set off in a run.

Mrs. Wellman on the other hand was totally focused on the groaning figure of James Woods. She bent over him and ascertained that he was still breathing. Then slowly and deliberately her hand stretched out to the abandoned garden hoe lying to one side of the patch of weeds. The lady was at the end of her tether, ever since they'd arrived at this posting David McCanles had been harassing them over the money he was owned (as if they could do anything about it), making threats. His temper and sense of injustice had grown even stronger after they had taken over the Ranch House and he had moved into the nearest town. She had had enough of the man, a man who had now come in to her house and physically assaulted her. She'd probably wear the scar on her cheek for the rest of her life. She needed retribution, she needed revenge, and she needed an outlet for her anger. But McCanles was dead. But the man that lay on the ground in front of her, James Woods, was one of McCanles' cronies. A suitable substitute. Her hand gripped the garden hoe, raised it over her head, and swung it down with all her might, frustration, and anger, onto the head of the wounded man. The resounding crack of the skull that followed gave her some sense of satisfaction.

So she tried it again, and again, and again. With Hickok off chasing the wounded Gordon, there was no-one to stop her rage. Eventually the adrenaline surge that was fueling her anger subsided, her arm was tired, and she lost her grip on the hoe that was now slick with blood and brain matter. The mess that had been James Woods' head was unrecognizable. She let the hoe fall, and dropped to her knees, sobs and uncontrollable shaking racking her body.

"Good God woman!" Horace Wellman's voice game from the porch above her. "What have you done?"

She looked up into the shocked face of her husband. "What you should have done." With that she stood up, brushed the detritus of her frenzied attack from her dress, and climbed the steps back to the porch, and passing her husband on her way back into the house said ,"Go help Hickok get the other one."

Horace Wellman, who was now carrying the shotgun that McCanles had assaulted his wife with, spotted the trail of blood that the wounded Gordon had left in his flight to find cover and started along it. As he reached the edge of the creek he heard Hickok's voice, "Wellman, stop, I can't hear nuthin' with your crashin' about."

Hickok appeared alongside the Station Manager and put his fingers to his lips to indicate silence. He stood still, listening for any sign of movement from within the reeds around the creek edges. Suddenly his back straightened and his head swiveled to his right, his head cocked over to one side as if to try and catch a sound on the wind. Wellman couldn't hear anything and raised his eyebrows quizzically. The only answer he got was Hickok reaching out his left hand and gesturing at the shotgun.

Wellman handed over the firearm and Hickok disappeared back into the bank of reeds as silently as he had emerged from them. Wellman listened intently trying to make out his stock-boy's passage through the undergrowth, but couldn't discern anything.

Then the creek bank reverberated to the sound of both barrels of a shotgun being unloaded.

Hickok reappeared handed the shotgun to Wellman with the command to "Stay here" and headed back toward the direction of the ranch house and station. When he returned he was carrying a spade and a blanket. He simply shrugged at Wellman and returned to the reed bed.

James Gordon was buried where he fell, simply wrapped in a blanket. James Woods and David McCanles were thrown into a large wooden box that had been dragged from the barn. The box was loaded onto a wagon and the former freight driver steered it in the direction of a local burial ground off the station property. The box was interred on Soldier Hill without ceremony.

Back at the station, Sandra Schulls wrapped her arms around the young

William McCanles, guided him to the front seat of her buggy, and drove into the nearest town to tell her story.

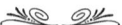

The posse arrived three days later. Ten men on horseback. Hickok thought that was a little excessive. It's not like he was going to run. If he had any thoughts or intentions of fleeing he had plenty of opportunity over the intervening days following the events. Instead he'd calmly returned to looking after the way station's horses and awaiting the arrival of the law that he knew would come for him.

He wasn't sure who they would send, but in the end it was the sheriff, his deputy, and a motley bunch of what Hickok took to be town's folk. "That's him, sheriff," one of the posse, a man that Hickok recognized as one of McCanles' crowd. "The one that done for David and the others."

Hickok let the rope bridle he'd been holding run from his hand as the horse he'd been working walked away. He made no attempt to follow and retrieve it. Let the animals run free, even if he wasn't going to be. He decided he no longer cared. Fate had arrived, and the Overland Stage Company, its property, horses, and shady business deals could go hang. Because there was a good chance that was going to happen to him, and sure as hell the company wasn't going to raise a finger to help him out this time around. Getting injured is one thing, gunning a man down on company property was another.

The ride into town was uncomfortable, mainly due to the ropes that they had used to bind his hands. The knot had been poorly done and it was pulled too tight, both rubbing against his skin and making it difficult to sit correctly on the horse he'd been placed upon. One of the sheriff's deputies held the reigns and led it into town.

As well as Hickok they'd arrested Horace Wellman, for the murders of McCanles and the two Jameses, but had left Mrs. Wellman stay free. Hickok wondered if Horace had said something to Sandra before she'd headed into town that fateful day. Was he prepared to take the blame for what his wife had done? On the day Hickok had thought that Wellman had behaved like a coward, but now his estimation of the man improved somewhat. Of course the true test would be when they appeared in court. What would Wellman say when there were witnesses who knew better. While Sandra had seen things from a distance, having stayed hidden in the barn, young William McCanles had seen the death of his father and the subsequent events first hand, up-close.

The town of Endicott, Nebraska lay about four miles from the Rock Creek way-station. It was little more than a collection of a few hastily constructed buildings scattered around a cross roads. Not yet large enough to boast of a purpose built courthouse, or a permanent resident judge, meant that the proceedings in the case against Hickok and Wellman would take place in the town's most frequented public space, the local saloon.

The ubiquitous circular tables had been stowed out back, with one exception, which had been placed in a position for the use of the traveling circuit court judge. The three day wait between the shoot-out and the arrests had been timed to coincide with the judge's arrival in town. The motley collection of mismatched, patched, repaired, and unstable chairs had been arranged to provide seats for the two accused to one side of the room, and a witness stand to the other. Across the room were two rows for spectators, and anyone not early enough to claim one of those would have to crowd in and stand. It was anticipated that most of the town, and folks from surrounding farms, would probably turn up as interest was high; and there wasn't much else going on in Endicott anyways. A fair cross section of the town folks were hoping for a lengthy trial to entertain them over the weeks to come, while another section wanted it to be over as quickly as possible so they could get back to drinking in the saloon. Its choice as the location for a temporary courtroom had not been a universally popular one. Hickok didn't really care either way; he just wanted to get proceedings going. If fate was to deal him a cruel blow, then he wanted to get it done, and be over with it.

One thing he did do to prepare was to follow Sandra's advice. He bathed, washed his hair, and got her to deliver his best clothing to the jail. He arrived in court looking fresh, neat, and smelling clean, with his long locks flowing down to his shoulders. The ladies of the town were impressed. This presentable, neat, and handsome young man couldn't be the stone cold killer that some people had been suggesting. Could he?

Hickok took a good look at the man who would make that decision. Judge William Pitt Kellogg was in his early thirties, and was clearly a man on the rise, having been recently appointed by the President as the Chief Justice for the state of Nebraska despite his young age. He was a tall, lean man, who sat with a confident pose of one sure of his station and purpose in life. The hairline was starting to recede slightly at the front giving him the appearance of a high forehead, which was contrasted at the opposite end of his face by a well groomed and shaped thick beard that was worn at the fashionable length, just covering the neck but not covering the shirt collar, which revealed a small neat bow-tie. His face was also lean, and his features suggested an inquisitive, yet empathic man lay beneath. Hickok believed that no matter which way the verdict went, that this man would ensure that the day's proceedings would be conducted with due process and fairness to all involved.

Once the formalities of the introductions had been announced, the charges were read by the local sheriff, "That the accused James Butler Hickok and Horace Wellman of the Overland Stage Company, employed at the Rock Creek Way Station, had maliciously murdered three men, to wit James Gordon, James Woods, and David McCanles noted citizens of the town of Endicott."

Hickok smiled at the use of the phrase 'noted citizens.' The sheriff hadn't been specific about what they were noted for.

The local postmaster, who had a few run-ins with McCanles himself over the years had been appointed by the company to act as the spokesman for the defense, and he did his best to present the shootings from Hickok and Wellmen's perspective. But he was less than effective as both storyteller and orator. As he sat down the sheriff stood and called to the stand a Mr. McCanles.

At first Hickok wasn't sure who he'd been referring to; as far as he was concerned the only Mr. McCanles he knew has lying in a box on Soldier Hill. The mystery was cleared up when young William McCanles entered. He looked nervous and scared. Not by Hickok, who he smiled at as he passed, but by the surroundings. He had been scrubbed clean, and dressed in a suit that was clearly too big for him to make him look older. Probably that was why he'd also been referred to as Mister when summoned.

The young boy stood shaking holding on to the back of the rickety chair that had been designated as the witness stand. Judge Kellogg leaned forward and lowered his voice. "What's your name?"

"Billy McCanles, …. Sir." The boy stammered back.

"And what's your relationship to the deceased?"

The boy looked puzzled. "The what now?"

"The men who were shot."

A light of understanding briefly passed across the boy's face, he quickly looked in the direction of the Sheriff, then it was quickly replaced by a mask of sadness, one that to Hickok's eyes looked rehearsed. It made him wonder just how upset the boy was at the loss of his father. "One of them was my pa."

"That would be David McCanles?"

"Yes, sir."

"And how old are you son?"

"I'm twelve…" the boy's voice caught in his throat, "…ah mean I'm fourteen, no sixteen."

"Now which is it, son? And remember no matter what anyone else has told you to say, this is a court of law, and you've got to tell the truth."

There was a moments silence as the boy looked around as if trying to find a familiar reassuring face. Then his chin dropped, and he stopped looking at the judge. "Twelve." He muttered.

The judge sat back up straight and addressed the court. "The McCanles boy is too young to give evidence. Any testimony he may give is inadmissible. Therefore he is relieved from testifying. The sheriff bolted from his chair, "But he's the only eye-witness to what happened out at Rock Creek."

The postmaster stood, crossed the few steps to stand before the judge, turned and looked at the sheriff with a gleam in his eye. "Oh no he ain't." He turned to the judge. "If it's OK with you Judge Kellogg, I'd like to invite Miss Sandra Schull to the witness stand."

The sheriff hissed, "You said you weren't going to call on her."

"Did I?" the postmaster responded with a look of pure innocence. Then he grinned.

The sheriff stood and shouted, "This ain't right Judge. That woman has been spreading her side of the story all around town for the last three days. She's Hickok's woman. She's biased."

"Are you objecting to her being called as a witness?" the judge responded.

"Sure as heck I am." The sheriff asserted.

"Overruled. It's my understanding that she was an eyewitness on the day of the shooting. And as such I'd like to hear her testimony."

Hickok felt a little surge of masculine pride to hear that Sandra was considered in town as 'Hickok's woman.' He also had some sympathy with the sheriff. He was right about Sandra. She had been telling her side of things to anyone who would listen. The way she told it Hickok and Wellman were protecting themselves from sudden attack. McCanles and the two men had gone to the station looking for trouble and were armed to scare Wellman and force the issue of payment for the property. She contested that Hickok had fired in self defense, and had no choice because it was three against one.

She told it the same way again. This time to the judge. Hickok liked the fact that she was consistent.

After she had finished the Judge retired for his deliberations, but given the short time he was away Hickok assumed that the deliberations had been little more than a quick trip to the out-house out back of the saloon.

"The defendants will rise." Judge Kellogg ordered.

Hickok and Wellman stood to await their fate. Wellman was clearly nervous and swaying a little. Beads of sweat were on his upper lip and brow. In contrast Hickok stood stock still, he was as calm as if he was about to take a Sunday afternoon stroll down main street.

"After listening to the testimony of the only reliable witness, as well as the arguments made by the town authorities, I have come to the conclusion that the shootings were an act of self defense in response to a potential violent confrontation. The court finds the defendants not guilty of the charge of willful murder."

The verdict was met with a lot of muttering from the various townsfolk ranged around the saloon. The judge held up his hand, and the noise abated. "Horace Wellman, I suggest that you and your quick-tempered wife discuss with your employers the benefits of another posting outside the state of Nebraska."

"Yes, sir." Wellman gulped. "I'll do that, sir. Thank you, sir."

"James Butler Hickok," the stern countenance of Judge Kellogg remained passive as he addressed the younger of the two men in front of him, "it seems that we have something in common. We are both Illinois men who find ourselves relocated here to Nebraska at the behest of others. In my case I am here at the request of Mr. Lincoln, while your presence is thanks to your superiors of the Overland Stage Company. "

The revelation of the common roots of the Judge and the recently acquitted man brought forth a few more murmurs from the spectators, not all of them appreciative of the co-incidence.

"I believe for both of us, that this may just be a temporary stopping point on life's journey," the judge, ignoring the mutterings of the crowd, continued, "I suggest that you should take advantage of your good fortune today to move on. We live in dark times, and have a divided country before us. A man of your wild temperament and quick guns could supply much needed talents to the defense of our nation."

"You're crazy coming here." Sandra Schull stood with her right arm hooked around Hickok's waist. "You heard the judge. He pretty much told you to get out of town."

"I heard him." Hickok turned towards her, gazed into her eyes with affection, "but I gotta do this first."

"The last thing you should be doing is getting into a confrontation with another McCanles."

"It won't come to that." He leaned forward and kissed her lightly on the forehead. Then he gently removed her arm from around his waist. "Wait here. I won't be long."

Hickok strode across the street towards the house they'd both been looking at. It as a well built two story property with a balustrade wrapped around the porch. The sort of house that spoke of being owned by a man of property. What marked this house out from the few other similar ones in Endicott was the black cloth draped around the front door and windows. Hickok stepped up into the porch and knocked on the black draped front door. After a short while it quietly swung open. A young boy stood there starring at Hickok. "Afternoon, Billy. Is your Ma at home?"

"Who is it?" Came a voice from the depths of the darkened house.

"It's Mr. Hickok."

"Well don't leave him standing there, show him in."

Hickok followed the young boy down the hall and was shown into the parlor. Standing in middle of the room was a woman Hickok judged to be in her mid-thirties, although the black dress and the gloomy room made it difficult to be too precise. She held out her hand in greeting. "What can I do for you, Mr. Hickok? It isn't everyday that the killer visits the widow."

Hickok took the offered hand and made a slight bow, "I came to offer my apologies, Mrs. McCanles."

"Apologies, Mr. Hickok." The lady seemed more bemused than shocked. "You now regret gunning down my husband?"

"To be honest, ma'm, no I do not. He was a bully, and deserved what he got."

"So what are you apologizing for, sir?"

"For leaving you and you son in need." He reached into his pocket and pulled out a crumpled bunch of bills. He reached out and presented it to the widow. "$35. Restitution to help you out. Sorry it ain't more, but it's all I have at the moment. I'll send more when I get it."

Mary McCanles laughed softly and with warmth. "Mr. Hickok I'm glad you killed that man. He was a bad husband, and a poor father." She looked at Billy and gestured him to her side, where she placed a protective arm around his shoulders. "Despite the issues at Rock Creek he was however a fair businessman. His various business partners have offered to ensure that we will have a fair income."

"Ah." Hickok dropped his arm feeling a little embarrassed.

"But none of them ever offered me everything. Keep your $35 young man. May it bring you fortune."

"Thank you, Ma'am." Hickok returned the crumpled bills to his pocket and turned to take his leave.

"It took a lot of guts to walk into this house, Mr. Hickok." the widow McCanles smiled, "Wild temperament. Isn't that what the Judge said? It suits you." She took his hand in hers, then leant forward and gave him a light kiss on the cheek, "Take care out there Wild Bill."

THE END

MUSINGS ON WILD BILL
Part One - Beginnings

The story you just read is true. Well most of it anyway. That is according to James Butler Hickok.

My first encounter with Wild Bill Hickok was the polished, clean-cut, singing version as portrayed by Howard Keel in the Doris Day musical *Calamity Jane.* As a consequence I never really took Hickok seriously. Sure I knew that the musical version wasn't anything close to the historical events, but there had to be some kernel of the original in there, didn't there? Hickok just wasn't my idea of a Western hero. I'm more of a Wyatt Earp guy.

A few years ago I was doing the research for a (as yet unpublished) graphic novel project centered around the friendship between Buffalo Bill Cody and *Dracula* author Bram Stoker (Yes, they knew each other), and Hickok's name kept popping up as someone Cody had met and admired. Maybe there was more to the man than I had previously thought.

Keith Carradine's portrayal of Hickok in the early episodes of the HBO *Deadwood* series cemented that this was a man with an interesting back story that the show could only hint at. Obviously given the historical timeline Hickok's involvement in the series had to be fatefully short. My interest was further piqued by a subsequent road trip visit to the city of Deadwood itself. But that was Hickok's destiny. What had bought him to that point?

The excellent 2019 biography *Wild Bill* by Tom Clavin (ISBN 978-1250173799) provided many of the answers, and also provided the inspiration for these stories.

And what better place to start than at the beginning? As I mentioned, James Butler Hickok stood by the basic facts of the tales presented here. The story of his encounter with the bear is one he repeated many times during his life, and aside from a few minor variations, told it pretty consistently. Of course there were no other witnesses to this event, other than the bear and pack horses, but what is known is that the young freight driver turned up in one of the towns on his route carrying fresh injuries that were consistent with a bear attack. And as a result of those injuries he was transferred to the Rock Creek station in Nebraska.

The events in Nebraska are a matter of public record to some extent, although there is conflicting versions of some of the details the basics are pretty consistent. We know that there was a dispute around payment for the purchase of the Rock Creek Station by the Overland Company from McCanles, and we know that it eventually led to a gunfight that left McCanles and two other men dead.

We also know that one of the central figures in that fight, who ended up being charged with the men's murder, was a young James Butler Hickok.

The participants and sequence of events in the Rock Creek gunfight presented here are pretty much in line with those outlined in the Clavin biography, with a few authorial embellishments. The only contemporary source as to what actually happened was the story told by Sandra Shull, and it's not even clear if she was there at the time, or had been coached by Hickok. Unlike in my version, she was never called to testify, but she had spent the time between the shootout and the trial telling her story around town. She kept telling the same story for the rest of her life, right up to her death in 1932 . A remarkable show of loyalty since Hickok apparently never bothered to contact her again after leaving Nebraska.

The only true witness to the events at the way station was McCanles' son, but, as in this story, he was deemed too young to testify, The actual trial took place in the town of Beatrice, the county seat of Gage County, Nebraska, But I liked the idea of moving it to the nearest small town with a circuit judge presiding. There doesn't seem to be any record of who the presiding judge was at the trial or where it was held. I made the assumption that it was probably a significant happening in the town closest to Rock Creek, which is now a Nebraska State Park. When I found Judge Kellogg during my research I just had to fit him in to the story. The gunfight fits alongside his presidential appointment as the Nebraska Chief Justice, a posting he didn't appear to be that enthusiastic about, but which proved to be a foundation of his subsequent political career. The parallels between his and Hickok's situation seemed too good to ignore.

Which sort of brings us back to Howard Keel. If there was one thing about the movie version of Hickok that they got right, it was his reputation as a snappy dresser. But that seems to have been a side of his character that developed over time. I thought that having Sandra tell him to clean up for his day in court would be nice starting point for his sartorial growth. The events of Rock Creek are perhaps the first recorded instance of his chivalrous attitude towards women, other than those he got romantically involved with, whom he seemed to abandon with regularity. Hickok's visit to the widow McCanles and offering her all the money he had is true, although some reports have him accompanied by another station employee and making the visit on the way to his trial, and an indication of the dichotomy of his character. He would become a killer with a conscience.

The Duck Bill nickname for Hickok was recorded as being used by McCanles as an insult, but having the widow McCanles transform it to the "Wild Bill" name is totally my invention. It seems that it was James Butler Hickok who came up with it himself during his time army service, and was popularized by a highly exaggerated retelling of the events of Rock Creek in an issue of *Harper's New Monthly Magazine* published in 1867, six years after the event. The article portrayed Hickok single-handedly killing nine desperadoes of the 'McCanles Gang" despite receiving 11 bullet wounds in the "greatest one man gunfight in history!"

Hickok may have wanted to slip away from Nebraska quietly and lose himself in the military, but the seeds of his legend had been sown.

BAT MASTERSON & ANNIE OAKLEY

"Masterson's Gamble"

by Teel James Glenn

When Bat Masterson woke that crisp October morning in 1902 he had absolutely no thought that he would shoot anyone by the end of the day, let alone a number of people.

Not that he wasn't in a mood to shoot someone as he sat in his office at the *New York Morning* Telegraph pounding away viscously with two fingers on his typewriter. His column for the day was railing against a bad judgment in a boxing match he has seen the night before and the words were sure to scorch a few eyebrows when they were read.

In the middle of a sentence impugning the ancestry of the referee there was a sharp female shriek from the hallway outside Bat's office. The mustachioed, middle-aged writer leapt up from his chair and raced to the door, pulling it open. What he saw was something that all but froze his blood.

In the center of the marble hallway there was a struggle going on between a petite woman and a burly thug. The man had the woman by her long hair, yanking hard on it while he brandished a vicious looking knife at her. "You were told to be quiet, wench," the man said with a snarl.

"None of that!" Masterson yelled. The knifeman only acknowledged the order with a glance. He raised the blade to menace the sports writer and point it at Bat with a guttural snarl. "This is none of your business, old man, butt out."

Masterson replied to the threat by reaching into a vest pocket to snap out a handy .32 revolver. He pointed it at the knifeman with deliberate care. "Let her go, my young friend or this 'old man' will let go lead."

The thug yanked on the woman's auburn hair again hard enough to pull the woman off her feet with a squeal of pain. "I'll kill her if…" knifeman began but never got to finish the sentence because Masterson put a bullet squarely through the man's right shoulder.

The attacker staggered back, the knife flying out of his hand and releasing the girl who dropped to her knees.

"I don't threaten, my young friend," Masterson said quietly. "I promise, and I don't repeat myself."

The released victim rose and scrambled out of the line of fire to head toward her savior. At the same time the wounded attacker staggered back to brace himself against a wall. His shoulder wound bled through his rough jacket and stained the brown an ugly dark color.

The attacker's hesitation gave the sportswriter a moment to take in the girl he had saved as she moved toward him. The first thing he noticed that she was no indolent Gibson girl.

There was a country-bred handsomeness to the girl's features. Though small in stature she was a full-grown woman who wore a homespun dress— well made to be sure—and there was also something vaguely familiar about her as well that tugged at the sport's writer's memory.

The woman smoothed down her waist-length hair and drew herself up to her full five feet with great dignity. "Mister Masterson, I need your help."

The gaslit hallway of the newspaper building was filling with people now emerging from their offices to investigate the commotion. The knifeman tried to use the confusion to escape, forcing himself on one of the typewriter girls who had spilled into the space. The girl screamed as he grabbed her arm with his good left hand.

Masterson wasted no time in a second warning to the attacker. He snapped off a shot without seeming to aim, this time putting a bullet directly through the man's forehead.

The typewriter girl the thug was holding pulled away as the man fell dead. The girl then screamed once and fainted away as the others who had come into the hall and began to cry out.

"I told him I don't repeat myself," Masterson said matter-of-factly as he re-pocketed his revolver.

He turned to the rescued girl still sure he had seen her before. "Come on into my office, Miss," he said. He raised his voice to address some of the stunned workers who stood gawking. "Get the police and get some brandy for Flo over there, looks like she could use it!"

Masterson entered his office after the girl, leaving the door ajar and grabbed his jacket from a coat rack to put on, both for propriety's sake. "Now Miss," the sportswriter said turning to face her, "What is this…"

"You don't remember me, do you, Mister Masterson," the petite woman asked, her voice with a soft southern accent. "Perhaps I can stir your memory if I said Kansas City?"

The mustachioed sportswriter looked at her with new eyes now and suddenly the memory returned. "Of course," he exclaimed, "that one time I stopped into Buffalo Bill's Wild West Show for some help from Mister Cody I saw you; no wonder I didn't recognize you as you are…"

"I know," she said with a shy blush, "I get all fancied up in those flashy duds I make special when I do my shootin' show."

"Miss Annie Oakley!" Masterson said with a wide grin.

The woman did a small curtsey. "On stage, yes; but Mrs. Frank Butler when not, Mister Masterson."

Though he had not actually met her, the sportswriter had seen her shooting act when he visited William Cody's '*Buffalo Bill's Wild West Show*.' She was a living legend for her amazing marksmanship with rifle or pistol, rumored to never miss! She had traveled with the Wild West show giving shooting displays all over America and Europe to cheering audiences that include many crown heads and world leaders.

"How can I help you, Mrs. Butler?" Masterson he adjusted his jacket and gave a small bow with his recognition of the extraordinary woman.

"Please call me Annie," she said.

"Then it is Bat," he said with an easy smile that belied the actions he had just taken in the hall. "But please, Annie, what is it I can do for you and what was that mess in the hall all about?"

The stalwart demeanor of the little woman cracked then and she gave a slight sob. "I would have normally taken care of it myself, but his city, and the shock, I fear…"

At that moment a freckle faced copyboy for the paper burst into the room. "Mister Masterson," the toe-headed boy exclaimed. "Mister Sudsberry called for them so the police are on the way."

"And how is Miss Flo doing, boy?"

"Oh, Mister Collins took her home, but she was looking okay when they left, sir." The boy looked over at the famous sharpshooter without recognition. "The police should be here in a few minutes, sir. Should I bring them in to…"

"Thank you, Toby," Masterson said. The boy stood for a moment, looking at Annie until the sportswriter arched an eyebrow and shooed the boy out with a wave of his hand.

"I can not deal with the police, Bat," Annie said. "It would be disastrous to do so at this time."

"What do you mean?"

In answer she thrust a crumpled piece of paper into Masterson's hand.

"This was in our hotel room when I returned there this morning," she said, "and I did not know what to do."

The paper had a crudely scrawled note on it that read, "If you want to see Frank Butler alive do not contact the police! Say nothing. Do nothing and wait in your hotel till you hear from us!"

"Your husband?"

"Yes; I had an early appointment with a doctor about my back; I had surgery last year on it, you know. I did not want to bother Frank so he stayed behind to have his breakfast." She sobbed again. "But when I got back no more than an hour later I found this note on the floor of the hotel suite. I didn't know what to do, or where to go in this big mess of a city. Then I remembered that you started your column with this newspaper recently and that my hotel was not far from here."

Masterson studied at the note with knit brows and nodded. "I agree going to the police is pointless. They are not far past Clubber Williams and his corrupt regime, despite what Teddy Roosevelt did with his reforms when he was police commissioner."

"I think that hooligan in the hallway must have followed me from The Park Avenue Hotel. That is where we are staying, to over here," she said. "He must have realized I was looking for help; though he could not have known I was coming to you."

"I am flattered, Annie," the sportswriter went to his desk and unlocked the bottom drawer from which he pulled out a shoulder holster with a .38 revolver and a box of ammunition. "I thought I was done with gun fights and fighting crime back in '81 in Dodge City." He got a pensive look on his face. "Not a thing I ever hoped to be tangled up in again."

She looked at him with great concern. "Does that mean…"

He smiled. "No worry, ma'am, I guess once a lawman, always a lawman." He took off his jacket after turning his back, donned the shoulder holster then re-donned the jacket.

"I'd feel better if I was heeled as well," Annie said quietly. "We aren't that much off the Tenderloin this far west on the island."

"I expect, you will feel better," he said and handed her his .32 and the box of ammunition. "I wish I had a better bit of artillery for you, Annie."

She hefted the pistol. "It'll do, Bat, least ways till I can fetch some of my own."

"Then, if I am to imitate John Law we had better take off before the real badges show up, ma'am."

"But what will we do?" She asked as she reloaded the .32 with a sure hand and placed it in a concealed pocket in her skirt. "Where do we start?" Her voice betrayed despair. He took note and smiled reassuringly.

"We go to your hotel first to see if there is any ransom demand." He pulled out the sheet from the typewriter that he had been working on and scrawled a few notes on it with a pencil. Then he gathered up the rest of the article had been working on and then went to the door, calling out, "Copyboy!"

Almost before he had finished calling young Toby magically appeared in the doorway.

"This goes to the typesetter, Toby," Masterson said as he handed off the article. "My last bit and the sign off is handwritten, but he can read my scrawl well enough." The boy looked past the pile of papers to stare at Annie again but Masterson added, "Scoot!" and the boy raced off.

"We can head out the back way," Masterson said, "and catch a hansom by the loading docks without running into the Billy-club boys." He grabbed his Derby hat and his walking stick and then gestured for the lady sharpshooter to precede him.

The two fugitives headed down the hallway, past the other offices, only stopping for the former lawman to lift the blanket that had been hastily thrown over the thug who had accosted Annie. He knelt down to search the man's body, going through the threadbare jacket and vest. He pulled out a wallet from an inside the jacket pocket and secreted it before leading the lady sharpshooter down the back stairs to the loading dock on Fifty First Street.

"Will the police not be after you for shooting that hooligan?" Annie asked as they walked out to the street and hailed a closed carriage.

They quickly climbed in and it pulled away from the loading dock of the newspaper in the late morning traffic to Park Avenue and then down to Thirty-Third Street.

"The police know me well enough from my interactions with them since I got here earlier this year. I had a few run-ins with them at a couple of fight events, it is true," he said as the carriage moved slowly across town to where the Park Avenue Hotel was located.

Masterson added, "But they also know I don't go ventilating people for no good reason. I expect they will not look too hard for me, expecting me to come to them, which I will, soon enough." He pulled out the dead man's wallet; it contained only a few dollars and the 'mate's papers for one Jason Flood and nothing else. "If the police can't identify Mister Flood it may delay word getting back to any confederates. And that could work in our favor."

"But that is taking so much of a gamble, Bat."

He smiled. "I'm used to gambling, Annie, but rest assured I will not endanger Mister Butler's life; any inquiries I make will be discrete." He held up the mate's papers. "These will, at least give us an avenue for back tracking that fellow if we find nothing useful at your hotel."

The detailed and ornate cast-iron façade of the Park Avenue Hotel on 33rd Street was an impressive sight rising five stories over the avenue as the two friends exited the carriage. The building that had been built in 1877, designed by architect John Kellum for a wealthy businessman who intended it to be a grand "Working Women" hotel for all the single ladies of the New York City's business community. It was not financially successful, however, so was soon rechristened as a luxury hotel to bring in new clientele.

The large lobby reflected that new intent with opulent oak woodwork and a high ceiling from which were suspended crystal chandeliers that cast a faceted light across the deep pile carpeting.

Annie went directly to the front desk to ask if there were any messages for her but there were none. There was a small noontime crowd in the lobby, some seated on couches in lively discussions, others admiring the artwork hung as an ad hoc gallery along the walls.

When Masterson saw the look of disappointment on her face when there was no message and felt compelled to say, "Don't lose heart; no one would go through this to take your husband just to hurt him, they could have done that in your rooms. There will be some larger purpose than simple thuggery in this and we will divine what it is and rescue him, I promise."

The statement did little to allay her fears but she tried to put on a brave face as they walked across the wide lobby to the steel cage elevator. Masterson stepped in beside her but his eyes were scanning the lobby behind them with the experienced observation of a former lawman.

"Don't let him see you looking, Annie but do you know that man seated at the couch near the side door, reading the paper," he spoke to Oakley in a low whisper and kept his expression neutral.

She peered past the sportswriter with a smile on her face as if she were laughing at some joke of his, secretly studying the man. It was clear the man studying her over the edge of his newspaper.

"No, I don't know him, Bat," she said as she turned away before it was obvious she was looking beyond him. "At least he does not look familiar to me."

"He has had eyes for only us since we entered the building," Masterson said with a clam tone. "He is a low type, a racing tout or gambler from the look of him."

"How can you tell?"

He smiled and gave a small laugh. "You forget I've spent a good deal of time at card tables and intuition on things like this can make the difference between winning and losing. One can see the look in the eyes, the attitude of the body, how they hold their head and look at the world. That and his interest in you was clearly not just casual."

"What should we do?"

"For the moment, nothing. If he is still here when we come down we will see."

"Fourth floor," the markswoman said to the elevator operator as they entered the cage. They slowly rose and the metal-framed cage allowed the two watch their observer until the lobby was out of sight when they reached her floor. The newspaper reader did not move while they observed him but he stopped pretending the read his paper as they rose.

"Let me go first," Masterson said when they arrived at the door of the Butler's suite, his hand in his coat resting on the butt of his revolver. She had her own pistol out as she slipped the key into the lock and stepped to the side of the door.

"I keep praying Frank is waiting and it has all been a nightmare I will wake up from."

Masterson nodded and pushed the door in, springing through and sliding to the right side of the door so he was not a target to anyone inside.

The room was empty and showed no signs of anything having been disturbed.

"It's okay, Annie," he called but kept his eyes scanning the room. She entered and pocketed her pistol.

She looked over the room and moved to a breakfront where some glasses and a breakfast tray were set. She searched it and her shoulders dropped. "No note," she said in a deflated tone. She collapsed onto a settee as all energy and hope seemed to go out of her.

"Don't lose heart, Annie," Masterson said. He walked to the door to the bedroom and repeated the lunge into the room, then poked into the clothes closet and washroom to be sure they were truly alone.

"We will find out what this is all about and find your Frank." He looked to the front door and squared his shoulders. "I'm an old bluffer from way back, Annie, I think maybe we need to have a little conversation with that fellah in the lobby before we make another move."

She nodded and sat up straight. "You're right, of course; but let me change first to some better clothes to be ready to do whatever has to be done." She bounded up like a teenager and moved passed him into the bedroom of the suite. "I will not be long, Bat."

Masterson went to the small bar across the room and made himself a short whiskey to brace for that was to come. He had no illusions that it would all work out well—there was one man dead already. Frank Butler had been taken by someone who was clearly ready to do Annie harm to protect whatever secret they had. It was clear those that took him were serious and the stakes as high as any he could imagine. There was likely to be more gunplay and even death in the day to come. The only hope was that Frank or Annie, or least pleasant prospect to contemplate, himself were not among the book of the dead register for the day.

But why? What percentage to take Frank Butler? Bat thought about all he knew about Annie's husband and his reputation; he had been the preeminent show marksman in the country till he lost a shooting contest by one shot to a sweet young Arkansas country girl twenty years before then had fallen in love with her.

Since then Frank had become Annie's manager and biggest supporter, often right beside her in shooting exhibitions traveling the country and even overseas to perform for the crown heads of Europe. Could the kidnappers have wanted to put pressure on Annie for some reason or was it about some slight or failing of Butler's? No rumors of Frank being a gambler had ever found their way to the underground sources of Bat's and Lord only knew there could be not chance of Annie's husband philandering. After all, who would cheat on a woman who could shoot the eye out of a bluejay at half a mile?

If the kidnappers wanted to pressure the young woman they had seriously misjudged her character. Bat was sure that the little sharpshooter from Arkansas was not a person to be forced to do anything she did not want to and there

...as all energy and hope seemed to go out of her he said, "Don't lose heart, Annie."

would be hail Columbia to pay when she found the ones who had taken Frank.

"Woolgathering, Bat?" Annie had changed into a traveling skirt and jacket in deep browns and had donned a long coat. He noticed she had also donned sturdy hiking boots.

No delicate fillie, this one, he thought.

"Just plotting and planning, Annie," he said. "We have to get ahead of anything they might spring on us."

"And?"

"I think I should head down the stairs while you follow in the elevator," he said. "If you cross the lobby and that tout follows you I shall follow him and ask him a few pointed questions."

"And if he does not?"

"If he ignores you" he smiled sheepishly, "then I had better not play cards for a while as I would have lost my critical faculties in my judgment of people."

"I have faith in your judgment, Bat." She stepped over to him and he was reminded again of how petite she was as she looked up to him and offered his small revolver back to him. "Thank you for the use of this."

"Don't you think—" he began but she pulled back her coat to reveal she had a six gun holstered comfortably on her hip. He realized it was why she had put on the coat, to cover the rig.

"I always feel a little better with my own iron on me," she said with a coy smile. "Frank says it's the only jewelry ever looks natural on me. If I had not been so upset before I would have grabbed it before I ran off to get you."

"Would have cheated me of the chance to play gallant for you, Ma'am," he said with a chuckle. He tucked the derringer in his vest pocket again, patting it to welcome it home. "'Cause you would have ventilated the fellow with dispatch."

The two of them left the suite and walked to the elevator side by side.

"Give me ten minutes to reach the lobby and then summon the elevator, Annie."

"And if that fellah down below don't take any interest in me?"

"I'll follow anyone else who does."

"And if no one does?"

"We'll jump that fence when we come to it," he said. "We will find your husband, that I do promise."

Bat went down the stairs two at a time till he was just above the first floor then slowed to move quietly down to the door to the lobby. While he caught his breath –and resolved to cut back on his cigars—he cracked the door from the stairwell to peer into the lobby. He was pleased to find he had a clear view across the expanse of the large space to where the newspaper reader was seated.

The reader was not even bothering to pretend with the paper now, clearly watching the two elevator cages while smoking a pipe. He only looked at his paper when the one opened and Annie stepped out.

So you are here for the lady, Bat thought, *we will see then what you can tell us when we have a little chat.*

The former lawman watched as the lady sharpshooter moved with apparent unconcern and no especial speed across the lobby to the front desk to ask if there were any messages and then there were none, she walked out the front door of the hotel.

The reader waited a few moments, eyes toward the other cage *Watching for me, eh, fellah?* Then when Masterson did not exit the second cage the man rose and followed Annie out.

Bat waited until the observer was completely out the door, watching to see if anyone else moved to follow either Annie or the reader, but when none did, he exited the stairwell. Bat moved quickly to the front entrance while keeping the man and Annie both in sight.

The sharpshooter had paused outside the hotel as if unsure whether or not to hail a hansom cab. She made a show of it as I had instructed her and was good about not looking back toward the hotel.

The reader worked to linger near the doorway unobserved where he could watch Annie. He puffed on his pipe with apparent unconcern, tapping it with a hand and relighting it with a strike-all match.

Masterson moved smoothly to the observer and between puffs jammed his revolver into the fellow's side. The man gasped and stood up straighter.

"Easy and quiet, my eagle-eyed friend," Bat said. "Or I will ventilate your liver."

Up close the observer was heavy set, round faced and had a drooping left eye and a slight scar bisecting his left eyebrow. He stiffened more when the sportswriter pressed the .32 hard into his back. He almost spit his pipe out of his mouth and bit down on it hard to stop that. He clearly realized it was a gun and did not even question that fact.

"You shoot me, pal," he said between clenched teeth. "And the law will be on you from the sound alone before I hit the ground." His voice had a slight lilt to it, pure shanty Irish. He did not sound too concerned that the gambler would shoot.

"Not this little thing," Bat said wiggling the tiny derringer against the man to emphasize the point. "Your fat gut will muffle the sound and I'll be long gone before you hit the sidewalk like a bag of suet."

The lady sharpshooter had seen the former lawman's move and moved in to the pair but was careful to keep up out of arm's length. "Gott'em, Bat. Did he tell you anything?"

"Not yet, but he will." The mustached sportswriter grinned. "Best get us a hansom to take us to a little more private area."

She move to comply and Bat saw the eyes of the chubby man show a new fear, a realization that he was solidly in his 'prey's' hands. The gambler reached around to subtly pat the pipe smoker down, finding not a gun, but a flick knife at easy reach in the man's waistcoat.

"You don't know what you're dealing with," the thug said with a little desperation creeping into his tone.

"Enlighten me then, my portly fellow," Masterson said. "It will save a lot of trouble for everyone and you tailor a lot of work patching the hole in this jacket." He emphasized the point by pushing the barrel of the revolver with more vigor into the man's kidney.

Before the man could make up his mind to confess his sins the sharpshooter had hailed a horse drawn conveyance. Bat close-walked the man up to it where Annie entered first. When she was settled she drew her revolver and leveled it at the observer.

The man clearly knew her reputation and offered no resistance as he climbed in to sit opposite her.

"Just drive down Fifth Avenue," Bat called to the driver when he had was in and seated beside the pipe smoking man. "We're in no hurry, driver."

Then he turned to the prisoner. "Or are we?"

"Let me put a bullet in his knee, Bat," Annie said with a sharp whisper. "He'll talk soon enough then."

The man's eyes went wide and he almost bit through the pipe stem.

"I don't think that will be necessary, Annie," Bat said with casual acceptance of her offer. "With what we learned from Jason Flood we really don't need this fellow for very much."

"Jason wouldn't ta…" The chubby crook said before he stopped himself. His good eye began to twitch and he looked from the grim faced Annie and the smiling Masterson.

The sharpshooter saw what Bat was trying and added, "But Mister Flood was in so much pain he might have lied, Bat. How can we trust what he said with a man in that kind of agony?"

"Pain?" The prisoner blanched.

"I think he was past lying at that point, Annie."

"Agony?" The pipe smoker had let it drop from his lips to the floor of the carriage but was frozen with fear and made no attempt to grab for it.

"We can take this fellow down to the docks," Bat continued, "and get rid of him there; doesn't really matter if he tells us where Frank is since we know now."

"Well if it don't matter what he says can I at least use him for target practice?" She said, "I fell a bit rusty and if he is a fair size for it."

"Wait a minute, ye don't have to be doin' no shootin'" the prisoner said. "I was just hired to watch you, ma'am, same as Jason. We didn't have nothing to do with taking Mister Butler, I swear."

"Don't swear in front of a lady," Bat said. "And don't lie, either."

"It is the truth, sir, it is." The heavyset thug was sweating profusely now, his facial tick intensifying so it looked like he was sending Morse Code. "Big Bill just hired us to keep an eye on the lady here and make sure she did not go to the police. When she took off Jason and I followed her but I lost her so I came back to the hotel."

"He's just jawin' to keep breathing," Annie said. "I say we let some air into him to help him"

"On my mother's soul I swear it is the truth." The Irish criminal was almost sobbing now his face all but in spasm with the exaggerated tick.

The sharpshooter looked to Bat and arched an eyebrow. "This Big Bill?" she asked. "Know who this fellow is talking about?"

"I know him," Bat said with a disgusted tone. "Big Bill Finger was one of the worst of the Five Points gang leaders that President Roosevelt all but put out of business when he was police commissioner. That was before he went on to be Governor. Bill Finger was convicted for some fancy shenanigans with a bank robbery where a guard was killed and served a stretch up the river in Sing Sing Prison."

"Then let's go gett'em!" She patted her revolver with an enthusiasm that made the prisoner squirm.

"Not that simple, Annie. His place in the 'Points is a fortress."

"Ain't no fortress I can't shoot my way into," the sharpshooter declared.

"But he ain't there, sir, ma'am," the heavy thug corrected, eagerly. "I mean, not no more."

"Where is he?" Bat asked.

"I don't know," the Irish man replied quickly, "I swear! Jason was the one what dealt with Bill and then he come and hired me."

"So only Jason knew?" Bat said.

"I swear on my mother, sir, you can ask Jason and he can tell you. Bill, he kept a low profile after he come back, all the fellas in the Points moved in on his old turf so he went somewhere else."

"Ask Jason, eh?" Bat said looking at Annie who sighed.

"See how easy that was, fellow" Bat said to the Irishman with a broad smile. "No pain, no trouble."

"So you'll let me go?" the prisoner said hopefully looking between his captors. "Annie?"

The sharpshooter tapped her holstered revolver. "You know the lay of the land, Bat so this is your call."

"Okay," he directed the prisoner, "When you wake up, you forget you ever saw us and disappear or I'll find you and plug you myself."

"Wake up?" The Irishman asked just as Bat launched a short, sharp right to the man's chin that put the lights out for him. The prisoner slumped over and began snoring.

"Nice punch," Annie approved. "But what do we do with him? And what do we do next?"

"We drop him on a corner on our way back to the hotel where you get off then I go to down to the piers downtown to the seaman's hall to see what I can pick up about Jason Flood."

"Hold it there, Mister Masterson," her tone became more formal. "I'm riding this horse all the way to the finish line. It's my Frank that's out there."

"It liable to be a hard ride, Annie, Big Bill was fury before he went up to prison for four years; he's a wounded animal now from what I've heard and wounded animals are the most dangerous."

"We're wasting time, Bat."

He touched the brim of his Derby in salute. "Yes ma'am, my mama taught me never to argue with a lady that has made up her mind." He opened the window to the driver.

"Head for the west side, driver. A stop on the next corner then down town, we are heading for the seaman's hall down by the South Street pier."

The unconscious thug was deposited at a street corner near 23rd Street with a note in his pocket warning him to leave town when he woke.

"You sure he will keep his mouth shut, Bat?" Annie asked when they exited the hansom cab near the Hudson River.

"Even if he decides he is more afraid of Big Bill than of me, Annie," the sportswriter explained as they walked toward the pier. "He can't know what we are going to do to be able to warn him."

"Because we don't know what we are going to do yet, right?"

"Right," the former lawman laughed. "I'm still playing hunches."

"You seem to know your way around this sort of thing, Bat, so I'll trust you on this."

"Sadly I know this sort of low life types all too well. And to that end let me do the talking at the seaman's hall."

She nodded ascent and the two walked out to the base of the long wharf.

The Seaman's Hall was down the block from Fraunces Tavern where Washington said goodbye to his troops on Pear Street at the lower tip of Manhattan Island only two blocks from the waterfront.

The two new friends debarked from their closed carriage several blocks north, across from the under construction Alexander Hamilton U.S. Custom House.

"I want us to walk from here," Bat said as he and Annie stepped down at the Bowling Green. The mass confusion of the federal building being put up to house the duty collection operations for the Port of New York meant that no one paid much notice to the unusual pair.

"You know this hall place, Bat?" Annie kept up with the gambler's long legged strides as they walked along with the Hudson River at their right. The small grassy area at the waters edge was full of strollers, some of them having wandered down the nearby Financial District to get a breath of fresh air from the waterfront.

"I've been in there a bit ago," he said, "I've covered a boxing match that went bad there. Actually it is actually a tavern itself that serves as a hiring hall where the mariners between ships can register and often pick up land lubber work."

"You think they will know anything about this Jason Flood?"

Bat adjusted his Derby with one hand while he tapped along the path with his cane. "I am afraid it is the only lead we have, but it is a good bet that if Flood was hired to play watchdog on you this would be where someone would have found him."

The two walked past Fraunces Tavern to a low building directly across from a pier had no sign save an anchor with broken chain hanging in front of it.

"You had better stay out here, Annie," the sportswriter said. "This is a rough place."

The petite sharpshooter smiled. "I'm an old mountain girl, Bat. I've been in a few saloons in my time—as an observer."

"People may not talk if..."

"I'll stay as observer here as well," she said. "I know this is your hunting grounds, but you might need back up. Besides, you can't live a little old gal like me out here on the cold, cruel streets." She made a point of letting her eyes stray to several rough looking types walking along the waterfront across the street.

"I surrender, but stay in the shadows and watch yourself."

"Will do, cowboy."

Surprisingly there were electric lights in the saloon, but stepping inside was almost literally day to night. The large barn-like room was all smoke and the lights were weak. I was full of drinkers even in midday and every one of them rough looking characters.

A huge bald headed black man with a gold earring in his left ear moved to block the door.

"No dames," the Nubian said. He spoke quietly but there was an implied threat in his tone.

"I want us to walk from here," Bat said.

"Can't say I didn't warn you, Annie," Bat whispered. She snickered.

"I haven't been called a dame in a long time," she said. Almost magically her six-gun was in her hand and thrust up under the chin of the giant. "I'm not sure I like it."

"Sorry, ma'am," the bouncer whispered. He did his best to smile with his eyes since he did not dare move any other muscles.

"I'll lurk here by the door," she said in a casual voice, re-holstering her pistol. "Me and my new friend will just have a nice chat."

Bat chuckled, squared his shoulders and stroke across the sawdust covered floor. He wound his way through the crowded tables.

All eyes turned to follow Masterson but if their stares affected him he showed no sign.

"Whiskey," he said with a wide smile as he bellied up to the bar. "Neat."

The rotund bartender who looked like he had spent most of his life at sea with a nut brown tan and an anchor tattoos on both is forearms, gave a toothy smile as he poured the drink. "You're out of your depth, Masterson. There are a lot of people in this bar that would like to sink you as much see you sail clear."

Bat threw the drink back with a sigh. "I know the odds, Burton."

"I would not give you odds, Masterson," the barkeep said. He grinned to show gapped death. "A lot of people lost money on that call."

"Lesson there is never bet if you can't afford to lose." The gambler put his back to the bar to survey the room.

"What do you want?"

"Jason Flood."

"What about him? He ain't here, you can see for yourself."

"Who can see anything in this haze? But I kind of knew he wasn't here. What I want to know where the fellow who pulls his strings is."

The obese barkeep shuddered and his eyes grew wide. "I don't know what you..."

Bat used his cane to poke the barkeep in the gut. "I do not have the time to trade I-don't-know-nothings' with you, Burton. Tell me where a fellah can find Big Bill these days."

The bartender's eyes darted to either side of the gambler. Bat reacted quickly jumping back from the bar just as two of the patron's grabbed for him.

The gambler danced back and snapped his cane like a whip to smack each of the men in the faces, knocking them to the floor.

The bartender reached under the bar and produced a shotgun and tried to point it at Bat but a shot rang out and the gun flew from his hands.

The bar fell silent.

"Well, Bat," Annie called from across the room, the gun smoking in her hand.

"Ask the gentleman your question again, I'm sure he'll be more forthcoming, lessen he wants a lead tattoo to add to that one."

Masterson suppressed a chuckle and turned back to Burton. "Well, you heard the little lady. Big Bill?"

The bartender held his bleeding right hand, cursed and hissed, "Weehawken, New Jersey. He couldn't push his way back into the 'Points so he set up shop over there."

"Address?"

"All I know is it is off Park Avenue. Ask Jason."

Bat sighed. "Not an option. Give me another." He pressed the cane into Burton's throat this time and pushed. "I am not bluffing."

"Steam launch," Burton hissed. "Pier at fifty Seventh Street. He keeps it there."

"See," Bat smiled, "that wasn't so hard to say. If you lied, you know I don't; bluff, I'll be back. See you around, big fellah."

The gambler very carefully backed across the saloon till he stood beside the little sharpshooter.

"Thank you for the back up, Annie."

"My pleasure. And now?"

"Back uptown to talk with another gent, then maybe a scenic trip to the country."

"Works for this country gal. I've seen your stomping ground, maybe I can show you some of mine."

"I will ask only once more, Annie," Bat said as the two of them debarked from the steam launch on the New Jersey shore across from Manhattan Island. They were on a pier that thrust out in to the Hudson from narrow strip of land below the Palisades Cliffs.

"Let me do this alone," Bat pleaded with an earnest tone. "Wait outside while I beard this lion, Finger, in his den; please!"

The ex-lawman had tried when to dissuade the sharpshooter when they had hijacked the steam launch at the Manhattan pier after they had forced the address out of the boat's owner before they crossed the choppy river to the Jersey mainland.

"Up that way is Hoboken," Bat pointed to the left. "And a looping road that leads up to the top of the cliff, but these stairs will be faster." Across the wide dirt road were a steep set of steps that made several landings back and forth and went up the sheer cliff. "They lead us directly up to the Weehawken bluff," he continued. "Big Bill Finger's place is up there somewhere."

They crossed the road to a staircase at the base of the cliff.

"Well, you can't say I ain't gettin' my exercise with you, Bat," she said, ignoring his request to stay. She looked up at the long staircase. "And I thought you city folks had it soft."

"That up that way the train tracks cross this river road," Bat continued his tour guide narration. "Lots of folks will get off there and take a carriage down this way to Hoboken; lots of theatres there these days for those that don't want to go into the noise of Manhattan."

The former lawman tried again to talk Annie out of coming ahead to assault Finger's headquarters on the long climb on the stairs up from the muddy base of cliff. He was no more successful with this last appeal than with the other two.

"You keep wasting time and breath," she said as she readjusted her holster to free it up for a quick draw when they arrived at the top of the Palisades cliff. She looked back across the river to look back the way they had come and brushed some hair out of her eyes. "If Frank is up here, I aim to get him out, so you can stop trying to be gallant and get down to business."

The top of the promontory showcased several mansions of the New York rich who wanted to be close to the big city. There was a spectacular view of the bustling metropolis across the river but Manhattan Island seemed a world away in the tree lined boulevard along the cliff edge.

"Just easing my conscience, ma'am," he added as they turned from the cliff edge to the dirt road called Park Avenue. The streets of the little hamlet of Weehawken 300 feet above sea level were a dramatic contrast to the made thoroughfares of Manhattan Island.

"And three times is all I got in me. You plumb wore me down."

"Your sure that fellah at the boat dock can be trusted, Bat?"

"Not particularly," he admitted as they walked along Park Avenue the castle-like water tower ahead of them that dominated the skyline. "But his description of your husband's kidnapping seemed accurate."

The red brick Weehawken Water Tower, built only in 1883, was on the border of the next small hamlet, Union City. The impressive structure was modeled after the Palazzo Vecchio in Florence Italy and stood one hundred and seventy feet high. It dominated the skyline, out of place in the surrounding semi-rural two story buildings and small sheds.

The streets were all but empty in the mid afternoon, with a single horse drawn delivery vehicle brining some furniture to one of the small shops along the road. Annie and Bat walked casually along the path seeming to just be ordinary couple out for a stroll.

"I suppose that is true," Annie said. "I just gotta hope word does not get back to this Finger fellow."

"It will take him a bit to find his way out of the closet we tied him in, Annie. I am pretty sure he wasn't lying about where Bill was to be found, either. It jibes with rumors that he had to get himself out of the Point's until he could build up his position again. I think whatever he has taken your husband for has something to do with him making a power play to get 'back on top.'"

The address they had been given was set just back from the cliff edge. It was an impressive three-story building with an acre of grounds with a low wrought iron fence cutting it off from the other houses.

The two new friends approached the land the house was on from inland side with great caution.

Bat fell into his tour guide role again. "Over there beyond those two buildings is where Burr shot Alexander Hamilton." The two walked with casual gestures with him indicating with a wave of his hand the area in the event anyone happened to be lookout out of one of the upper windows of Finger's mansion. "This whole bluff used to be the place for duels; law wasn't so particular about shootings on this side of the river so the upper crust who felt compelled to settle arguments in a formal way with a pistol or sword would come over here."

The edge of the bluff was just beyond a cobble stone street that ran in front of the mansion they were interested in. Three hundred feet below was the coast road and the pier they had tied up their launch.

Bat led the two of them a copse of bushes, which would keep them hidden while watching Bill Finger's mansion. They crouched down to peer through the undergrowth.

"Well if'n I find the fellah's that took my Frank," Annie promised as she moved a branch to get the lay of the land around the mansion, "gonna be a sight more shooting going on."

Despite the circumstance Masterson chuckled. "Remind me again to never cross a lady from Arkansas."

"That's yer first mistake, Bat." She gave him a sly smile. "I ain't no lady."

The two watched the house for a short time, noting that there were guards patrolling the grounds at regular intervals, but with that regularity it was clear to see the ones they saw were not very alert.

"Also no dogs," Bat noted, "that will work in our favor."

"You planning to Indian sneak in?" She was obviously pleased that he used 'our' in discussing strategy.

"You will, Annie. I see another way for me," the sportswriter stood up and stretched. She looked at him with a curious expression.

"If we get caught going in shooting," he elaborated, "and if Frank is in there, he could take a bullet."

"Yes, I figured that, but what do you mean another way for you?" Her tone showed some doubt that she believed he had been honest with her.

"Bill Finger happens to know me and I know him," Bat said. Now she looked cross.

"What are you saying, Bat? You in this with me or not?"

"I met him two years ago when I was up at Sing Sing to visit an old friend— who was himself in jail there—I told you I have a number of contacts on the wrong side of the tracks. Well, in any case, when I first got to New York I went to look up my old acquaintance from across the card table. I was introduced to Bill then in a nodding way. I never forgot it, and I am sure he will not have forgotten me."

"So?" She tapped her foot with impatience and her fingers drummed on the butt of her holstered six-shooter which, with her history, was a threatening gesture. Bat smiled and held up a hand.

"I'm on your side, Ma'am, Remember?" He tapped his cane on his Derby. "If I go in through the front door as casual as can be I hope to be able to spot where they have Frank. There is no way Bill have any idea I'm in this hand of poker with you and Frank."

She considered what he was saying for a moment then nodded. "Sticking your neck on the block by doing that, Bat. We don't know what all this is about."

"Another reason for me to go in there, Annie, as I am a curious cuss." He adjusted his Derby hat, straightened his vest and smiled. "And if I can figure out it there is a safe way to get to your husband I'll make enough of a racket so you can hear and it should be a bit easier for you to sneak in."

"You really are a gambler."

"Some say I am. Some even say I am reckless, but I like to think that means I'm not a daredevil; I figure the odds and, well, maybe sometimes I run a bluff, but in this case I think this is the plan with the best chance of success."

"It is a plan," she agreed with a girlish giggle. "Not a great one, but I suppose it will have to do." She reached over to rest a hand on his arm. "I can not thank you…"

"Posh," he stopped her with a wave of his cane. "This is what friends do; and I am a gambler, after all, Miss Annie Oakley."

She leaned up and gave him a quick kiss on the cheek.

Before she could see him blush at the gesture he stepped out from the concealing bushes and strode down the street around the border of the fence to the main gate of the grounds of the mansion. He whistled a popular tune and stopped only to knock on the gate with his cane before slipping the cane through the grate to slip up the bar that closed the portal.

When he stepped onto the grounds two Winchester carrying guards appeared from behind some bushes immediately to confront him.

"We don't like no peddlers," one of the pug uglies challenged him

"That's good for me then, since I'm not a peddler." Bat made much of adjusting a cufflink on the wrist of the hand that held his cane.

"A smart one, eh?'

"I like to think so."

"You lost then, mister?" The thug asked in a way that said violence was coming.
Bat smiled. "No."

"Yes you are," the tallest of the two men said. He was a fellow with a scarred visage and a multiply broken nose that spoke of a long history in bar fights. "You are very lost, so step back outside that gate and leave now while you can still walk."

The second guard was a thin thug who had oversized fists that showed as many scars as his colleague's face. He gave a high-pitched laugh at the first's statement but it was cut off abruptly when Bat's walking stick slammed into his the center of his forehead.

The first thug tried to raise his rifle but the former lawman was as quick with his fists as most of the fighters he wrote about and hit Scarface with three lightning jabs with his left fist and finished him with a baseball swing of the cane.

The two guards had not hit the ground before three others appeared and came running from the other side of the mansion. The three all had guns pointed at Bat, hammers cocked.

"Hi boys," Bat said in a loud cherry voice. "You can tell Big Bill Finger that Bat Masterson has come calling on him with a smile on my face and a song in my heart; he'll remember me, I'm sure."

The guards came up short guns pointed at him but eased the hammers down. They all recognized his name, even though none of them had ever seen Masterson before.

While the guards focused on him Bat saw the diminutive sharpshooter hop over the fence to the side of the house and slip up to the back of the house where she flatten herself against the building. He made sure none of the guards saw where his eyes had strayed and returned his gaze to look them steadily in the face.

"You ain't Bat Masterson," one of the guards with a long neck and big Adam's apple said in a squeaky voice. "He's gotta be a bigger guy than you."

"Nah," another guard said, this one all shoulders and no neck. "He's a little guy, and a not an old guy like this Toff."

"How in the name of blazes did Finger hire such fools?" Bat said aloud with disgust in his voice.

"I have no idea," thin voice called from a second story balcony. "Except to say good help is hard to get these days."

The guards all stiffened and fear flashed across their faces. There was no one visible beyond the railing of the balcony but it was clear it was the 'boss' voice.

"You lost then, mister?" The thug asked with malice.
Bat smiled. "No."

"That is Masterson, you idiots!" the voice called. "Search him and bring him up here! Now!"

Two of the armed men kept their guns trained on Masterson while a third stepped forward—careful not to get in the line of fire of the other guards—and patted the sportswriter down, taking his walking stick, shoulder holstered revolver and the .32 caliber from his vest pocket. He kept his fear filled eyes locked with the ex-lawman who kept a genial smile the entire time.

"When your two friends wake up," Bat said as he was ushered into the entrance of the mansion. "You can tell them they've met fame; they can consider their bruises my autograph."

The mansion was reached by a set of wide steps flanked by two bronze Chinese lion-dogs that looked like they were sticking their tongues out at visitors. Bat returned the favor, an action that made 'Adams apple' give a high-pitched laugh.

Inside the building was a spacious foyer with a drawing room off to the left and a book-lined study visible to the right through partially closed sliding oak doors. Ahead in the entrance was a wide, carpeted staircase. It was up these steps straight ahead that the captive was marched, rifles at his back.

All the furnishings and fixtures had the sheen of being newly purchased and were of top quality to the point of ostentatious.

Bat kept his pace leisurely, not allowing the gunmen behind him to dictate his speed and while outwardly he was relaxed the ex-lawman was like a cat with that appearance, ready to move in a moment. All his senses alert as he scanned all he could see for any sign that Frank Butler might be in the building. He saw none but did notice a door to the side of the staircase that had a lock on it.

"*That is interesting,*" he thought, "*Could be something.*"

"Move," the thick-necked gunman prodded Bat with a rifle tip. This made the gambler stop and look over his shoulder with focused eyes.

"You do that again, son," Masterson said, "And you're gonna need a doctor to remove it from your behind."

The thug actually took a step back at the gambler's glare. Bat then smiled.

"Hurry up you buffoons," the thin voice came from a room at the end of the second floor corridor. "I want to know what brings that tin horn gambler out here."

"Not to worry, Bill, on the way up," Bat called up in a relaxed tone. "Be right there."

At the end of the upper hallway a door was open and Bat was escorted through into a large bedchamber. The room overlooked the front of the house through two wide French doors. In the center of the expensively furnished room was a man in a wheelchair flanked by two burly men and a tall, pretty blonde woman.

The man in the chair was a bizarre sight.

It was clear that standing he would have been a tall man, broad shouldered fellow with an exploding shock of white-blond hair and a bushy white mustache. They were the only features of him, however, that were robust for the man's features and arms were withered, his legs beneath the lap blanket thin in the extreme.

Masterson stopped just inside the doorway and took of his Derby, to hold it in both hands.

"I see the look on your face, Masterson," the man in the chair said. "A mixture of shock and pity. It is clear: don't try to deny it."

"I wouldn't think of lying to you, Big Bill Finger," Bat replied. "I had heard you were sick, that much made it back to the streets after you got out."

"They let me out early on a mercy release," Finger said with a watery laugh. "Just after I saw you up at Sing Sing I caught a lung ailment." He coughed a wet, hacking cough that shook his whole body and lasted for a long minute. His whole desiccated body

When he was done with the fit he fixed his eyes, which still had some of the fire of his old self in them as he said, "So what are you doing out here, Masterson? There are no fights for you to cover out here in Jersey."

Bat recovered form his initial shocked reaction and moved into the room but cautiously, because he could see the bulges of shoulder holsters of the two men who stood by the crime boss. He worked to keep his body relaxed and his outward attitude casual.

"Well, no fights worth me covering anyway if those boys of yours downstairs are any indication," Bat said with an easy grin.

"I said no horse feathers, Masterson," the desiccated gangster hissed. "Why are you here?"

"I was out here looking for a story and heard rumors someone was hiring some extra muscle and that got me a bit curious."

The crime boss squinted at Bat's statement and tilted his head to the side like a dog listening for a whistle. "I stopped my boys from ventilating holes in you down there to see what the hell you wanted; now I don't care. I don't like liars." He looked up at the two thugs on either side of him Masterson. "Take him out and get rid of him."

The men behind Bat reached for the sportswriter's arms but he took a small step forward. "Why did you take Frank Butler, Bill? What possible good could that do you?"

Bill held a hand up to stop the two thugs. "What do you have to do with Frank Butler, Masterson? Why would you think I would want that Wild West show peacock for anything?"

"Now who is talking horse feathers, Bill? That's my question to you."

"I can just make you disappear, gambler," Bills warned. "I don't need to take any jaw jacking from you."

"Not to blow my own horn, Bill, but you know two famous people disappearing at once will draw a lot of attention your way."

The wheelchair bound man rolled forward at Bat so swiftly that his two guards had to rush to catch up. He rolled directly up to the prisoner's feet and stared up at Bat.

There was still fire in the eyes of the desiccated gangster. "Tell me what you know."

"Or what?" Bat wasn't the least bit ruffled by the reedy voiced man. "You were gonna dump me in the river a moment ago anyway."

"You can go over the cliff in one whole chunk or in pieces, gambler. And you can be alive when my boys cut you up."

"I don't bluff, Bill," Bat said with a calm, firm voice. "But I do trade, you tell me why you took Butler and I tell you how I tricked on to the fact that you did."

Finger gave a laugh that turned into another deep cough that it took him a moment to recover. "Suppose you welch?"

Bat leaned down so that he was nose to nose with the seated man, which caused the bodyguards to crowd in. "You call me a four flusher again and I will tear your head from your body with my bare hands; I don't threaten—I promise."

The woman with Finger quickly pulled his wheelchair back but Finger showed no fear.

"Same here," the gang boss retorted. "So you go on to your heavenly reward easy then, Masterson."

"But only if I know why."

Finger laughed, this time without launching into a cough. "Simple, gambler, I needed a damn good shot."

"And so you kidnapped a famous rifle expert? That is a bit extreme even for you, Big Bill."

"It's a hard shot," the wheelchair bound man said. "None of the chuckleheads who work for me could make it and the so-called local experts all said it couldn't be done."

"What shot is hard enough to want risking the world knowing you kidnapped a famous man? For a garden variety murder?" Bat paced a little as he talked but angled himself so the four guns it he room could not shoot at him without endangering their employer.

"Really Bill," he continued, "you have enough muscle to have anyone taken out any time you want." Bat looked around at the guards. "But then again, I can see you do get what you pay for."

This last jab seemed to annoy the gang boss and he sneered. "I want the man who did this to me dead."

This statement made Bat gasp. "You can't mean…"

"That son of dog Roosevelt did this to me with those damn reform movements," Finger spit. "He put me away when I had the island in the palm of my hand and I caught this thing lung up there in that hellhole."

"You can't kill the President of the United States!"

"I damn well can!" The gang boss pushed on the chair arms and for a moment it looked like his rage might propel him out his seat. "I damn well will."

"That is insane, Bill," Bat said quietly. "You can't be serious, besides the president is protected by the secret service in Washington."

The crippled gangster pointed out the window. "That bloated, self righteous fool will be coming to attend a friend's wedding at a theatre in Hoboken today. He will take a train to up the road and will motorcade down that coastal road right below us. I just got the word last night, which is why I had to rush this." Finger was gleeful now his voice with more energy than he had shown the entire time Masterson had been with him.

"After McKinley was shot Teddy's security will not let anyone get near him." Big Bill continued. "But it is fate that I had my house here. Out there, not far from where Burr killed Hamilton, Frank Butler will have a perfect line of sight off my balcony to the car on the road below. I could not have planned a place and an opportunity more perfectly."

"You're mad, Bill. You can't make Butler make that shot."

"I can if he thinks his wife will die if he doesn't," Finger added. "I have my men on her in the city. Butler thinks I have her; it's how I got him."

"There is no where you can hide if you do that, Bill."

"What difference? I have no life; what can they do, put me in a jail cell? I'm a dead man and all that is holding me upright is my hate for that bull moose blue nose."

"You'll hang, regardless."

"I'll be dead before I can come to trial, gambler, which is why it has to be now, here, today."

"You're memory will be reviled for all time."

"What do I care? This is all there is and I want to go to the grave knowing that prig is in hell ahead of me." The gang boss' expression changed, from dreaming of vengeance to all business. "Now you pay up, why are you out here? On this day, particularly?"

Bat laughed. "All on you, Big Bill. I had no interest in you at all, really barely aware that you were even back outside till this morning."

"So why are you here?"

Before Bat could answer the woman pushing Finger's chair said, "It is time, Billy, Roosevelt's train will have arrived up the line by now."

"You're a lucky man, gambler," Bill smiled. "You get to be here for when history is made before you die. You can make good on your bet while we get things set up." He looked to one of the guards behind Bat. "Go get him up here."

"Frank Butler is in the house?" Bat blurted. *So he was in here, I have to find a way to get word to Annie.*

"Of course," Finger answered. "Now, sportswriter, how did you end up here?"

"Frank Butler," Bat said with an ironic smile. "He is the reason I'm here. I came to find him."

"What, why?"

There was a sudden sharp reports from somewhere down the corridor. Pistol shots.

The guard behind Bat turned to react and that was when the ex-lawman acted. He flung his Derby into the face of one of wheelchair guards and leapt forward to drive a fist that held a derringer that had been concealed in the Derby into the face of the other.

Before the first guard could swat the hat aside Bat aimed the derringer directly into Finger's face. He cocked the hammer.

"Stop your other boys," Bat told him in a low, clam voice, "or I'll turn your head into a sieve, Bill. And you know this is no bluff."

The guard from the doorway froze, as did the wheelchair guard, but the woman reached for the derringer in Bat's hand.

"Don't, Dorothy," Finger yelled. "He means it." The girl froze.

"Thank you ma'am," Bat grinned. "I ain't never shot a lady and I'd hate to start now."

"That ain't no lady, Bat," the voice of Annie Oakley came from out in the hall. The little sharpshooter came into the room, six-gun in hand, motioning the door guard out of the way. Behind her came a stout mustached man, limping and rubbing his wrist. "She was the Jezebel floozy that lured my Frank out of our room with a call for help."

"Seems to be the day for damsel rescuing," Bat commented.

Annie, holstered her six-gun and marched past the sport writer directly up to the tall blonde. Without a word Annie jumped up and launched a right cross that connected with the blonde's jaw and felled the woman instantly.

"She also ain't no damsel; no gal lies to my Frank."

Bat looked over at Butler who had disarmed the door guard and hefted the man's rifle. "Nice meet you, Mister Butler."

"Frank, please." The male sharpshooter stood along side the slightly taller, broader Masterson and kept Finger's guards covered with the Winchester. "Isn't my Little Sureshot something?" He had a wide smile on his face as he watched his wife.

Big Bill Finger was less impressed with the petite spitfire and pulled a pistol from beneath his lap blanket that he pointed at Bat. "I will not let a tinhorn cheat me of my revenge!"

Annie Oakley drew and fired from the hip in an eye-blink shooting the gun out of Bill's hand with an explosion of metal. It was perfect shot.

At the same moment Bat jumped forward and kicked the seated man in the chest which sent the wheelchair sailing across the room, out the French doors into the railing on the balcony where a tripod mounted rifle had been preset.

Finger slammed into the rifle and then the railing, which he went right through.

The gang boss never screamed, falling in silence with the rifle, to the brick walk below in front of the mansion. His neck snapped with the impact.

"I told you I didn't repeat myself, Bill," Bat he looked down on the body. The rifle with the scope that he had planned to use for his revenge rested across his chest.

Bat shrugged as if to shake off a chill then turned to the lady sharpshooter and her husband.

"Thank you, Annie. Mighty fine shooting, ma'am."

"My pleasure, Bat. What do we do about the rest of these varmints in here?"

"I expect we can find us a sheriff out here somewhere. Then maybe let President Roosevelt know how close he came to being a clay pigeon."

"I expect both of those things would be a good idea," Frank Butler said as he hugged his wife while keeping his rifle pointed at the thugs who stood against the wall of the room looking a bit stunned at the turn of events.

"Think he might be a bit grateful to you for it, Bat," Annie suggested. "Might even make you a marshal or some such, I hear he's a grateful sort of fellah."

"Sure be nice," Bat mused. "I was always a bit jealous of Wyatt when he got his badge. Yup, and that's worth repeating sure would be nice."

THE END

AUTHOR'S NOTE:

President Theodore Roosevelt had Bat Masterson's appointment a U.S. Deputy Marshal for the Southern District of New York! On February 2, 1905, the President sent Bat a letter which said, in part: *"You must be careful not to gamble or do anything while you are a public officer which might afford opportunity to your enemies and my critics to say that your appointment was improper."*

President Taft, Roosevelt's successor had his attorney general conduct an investigation of Masterson's employment, which resulted in Masterson being terminated on August 1, 1909.

For the remaining 12 years of his life, Masterson covered the major boxing events of that era for the New York Morning Telegraph.

Teel James Glenn—has stories have been printed in magazines from *Weird Tales, Spinetingler, SciFan, Mad, Black Belt, Fantasy Tales, Pulp Empire, Sherlock Holmes Mystery, SciFan, Sixgun Western, Crimson Streets, Silver Blade Quarterly, Tales of Old, Blazing Adventures* and scores of other publications and dozens of books and anthologies in many genres. His short story "The Clockwork Nutcracker" won best steampunk story for 2013 from Preditor and Editors poll.

He is also the winner of the 2012 Pulp Ark Award for Best Author, his website is: TheUrbanSwasbuckler.com

WILD BILL HICKOK

"Alamo Reflex"

by Alan J. Porter

Abilene, Kansas. 1871

The gambler picked up the fifth card from the baize table top where it had been thrown face down by the dealer. It felt slick and slightly cold in his well manicured hands. Slowly he turned the card toward him as he slid it alongside the four other cards already fanned out in his left hand. The nine of diamonds. Useless, it didn't add any value to the cards he already had, but he still reckoned that he had a winning hand. The other players studied him in the vain hope that he would betray some tell tale sign that indicated his reaction to the card he'd been dealt.

They were out of luck. The gambler watched as the other men at the table declared their hands, some were worthless, others fair, but none could beat what he held. He quietly laid the fanned out cards on the table and waited a few beats before speaking. "Two pair, aces and eights." For the first time that evening he smiled, "I believe the evening is mine, gentlemen." He pushed his chair back against the wall behind him, stood and scooped up the assorted coinage from the table, "Now if you'll excuse me, I have to go to work."

The gambler checked his route from the table to the door, then did a quick visual check around the rest of the saloon. The Alamo was an impressive place, considered by many, including the gambler himself, to be the most elaborate in Abilene, if not in the whole state of Kansas. How many other establishments boasted their own orchestra? The gambler appreciated the fact that they were there, and even if he didn't always like their repertoire on many evenings it added a touch of class and sophistication that he had always aspired to. There were two bars, and he favored being sat near the rear one so he could use the large mirror above it to keep an eye on happenings at the many gambling tables spread across the extensive floor plan. The second bar, which attracted the most patrons, probably due to the paintings that imitated Renaissance nudes hanging nearby, was more ornate with its polished brass rails and fixtures.

Satisfied that all was well in the establishment the gambler headed for one of the three double glass doors that were strategically placed along the Alamo's forty foot frontage. Once through the doors the gambler ignored the raised wooden sidewalk of Cedar Street and stepped into the dirt road. Once he reached the center of the street he brushed his long Prince Albert style coat back to clear the butts of his twin Colt revolvers, and tucked the sawn-off shotgun he had been carrying under his arm.

The gambler was gone; it was time for the city marshal to start his rounds.

The marshal cut an impressive figure at just over six feet in height, and carrying about one hundred and seventy five pounds in weight. He always stood stock straight, and few things escaped the notice of his piercing blue eyes. His distinctive features and aquiline nose were framed by a flowing mustache and long brown wavy hair that came down to his shoulders.

His physical deportment was emphasized by his like of fine cut clothes, for as well as the Prince Albert coat he habitually wore checked trousers and an embroidered waist coat, and on his head a low crowned wide black hat. Occasionally the ensemble would be completed by a cape lined with scarlet silk.

But perhaps the most startling thing about this impressive figure of a man wasn't his stature, or his clothes; it was his reputation.

If pushed James Butler Hickok would say that he only ever killed those that were worth killing. In the War of the States that had meant Confederate soldiers, afterwards it was those who meant harm to either himself or an innocent life, and of course killing Indians was permissible at any point.

Soap. It all started because of soap. Not only was the marshal a paragon of fashionable dress, the ladies of Abilene often mentioned to each other how his lengthy hair was always noted to be clean, and his complexion fair. Many said this fair complexion was a result of his rumored habit of bathing every day. Something that set him apart from other men in the tough cattle towns of the frontier west.

So it was that James Hickok's consumption of soap was prodigious and matched that of the town's only beauty parlor. In the various saloon bars many men made lewd remarks about his habit of cleanliness, and fresh smelling, smooth countenance, but never when the man himself was in the vicinity. Not if they wanted to live.

It was a shortage of soap that first bought Hickok to cross the transom of the Kent's Mercantile store a week or two after his arrival in town. Being as it was his first visit to the establishment, after greeting Mr. Kent and introducing himself Hickok decided to peruse the shelves to ascertain the full range of goods stocked by the store.

When the robbers entered the store Hickok was in the far corner, sizing up some cloth that might make a suitable new waist coat, hidden from view of the doorway by a stack of molasses barrels.

In retrospect calling the pair of miscreants 'robbers' was perhaps giving them too much credit. The pair were clothed in ensembles of dusty, torn, and filthy shirts and pants that looked like they'd been striped from dead men and worn for weeks across the desert (which probably wasn't far from the truth). The larger of the pair slapped the dust from his clothes and with a show of bravado strode up to the counter, "You the owner of this place?"

"I am indeed. Brian Kent at your service. How may I help you?" Came the calm response. The store keeper stood an impressive six foot and was well muscled from lifting and carrying the various barrels and sacks that his stock was invariably received in. He had seen a lot in his travels before settling down with a family to try his hand as a store keeper. He didn't scare easily.

"By handing over your cash, while my friend here," the robber gestured back to his friend, "helps himself to whatever we fancies." To emphasize his point the man drew a pistol and waved it around in front of the storekeeper.

"I don't think I can do that." Brian Kent replied.

This took the thief so what by surprise, "Why not?"

"Because I wouldn't like it." The new voice came from the corner of the store.

The thief turned and looked at the newcomer, taking in the immaculate clothes and the long hair, "And who might you be." He asked.

"Hickok."

"Th... th...that's Wild Bill..." came a stammer from the smaller thief, who was already making a fast track towards the door.

"That true?" The braver of the two asked.

"Yep." Brian Kent confirmed.

The pistol fell from the thief's hand and fell with a dull thud to the store's floor. "So sorry to disturb you. Didn't mean anything by it...." the thief turned and ran after his compatriot out of the door and down the street.

Hickok walked over, picked up the discarded pistol and laid it on the counter. The gun was old, rusted, and useless. "Souvenir for you." He smiled at the storekeeper.

"Thanks, Mr. Hickok."

"I didn't do nothing."

"You were here, that was enough. I'd like to repay you some way. How'd you like to join me and my family for supper this evening? It's the least I could do, and Mrs. Kent is a fine baker."

"Sounds like a mighty fine offer to me." Both Hickok and Kent turned to look at the newest arrival just stepping into the store. "And he ain't lying about Mrs. Kent's baking either. It's a well known fact around town."

"Thanks, Mike." Brian Kent beamed with pride at the confirmation of his wife's talents in the kitchen. He raised his arm to indicate the newcomer, "Mr. Hickok, I'd like you to meet Mike Williams. He helps run the city jail."

Williams reached out and shook Hickok by the hand. "Do I need to accommodate the two I just saw high-tailing it out of here?"

Kent laughed, "I don't believe so, Mike." He gestured towards Hickok, "Now they know that Will Bill's in town, I don't think they'll stop till they reach Kansas City."

"Good to know you, Mike." Hickok smiled, tipped his hat and left the store.

Williams watched him go with interest.

"What you thinking, Mike?" Kent asked.

"I think we may have just solved this town's cowboy problem."

Hickok smiled to himself, this might be an opportunity. He'd heard the exchange as he'd left the store. Being famous might have some benefits after all. He was starting to grow weary of being the target for mainly ambitious, and occasionally psychotic, gunmen. They may have made the occasional play to make a name for themselves at his expense, but none had succeeded. Yet. Abilene was coming almost as infamous as he was, and at the age of thirty-four, the idea of taming such a place appealed. It suited his ego. He could wear a badge again if, he smiled again, no when, they asked him. Especially if it came with a salary and a few bounties along the way. Will Bill Hickok was the man for the job.

The Texan strolled down the street, as he had done on each day since his arrival. When he settled in Abilene the young cowhand seemed no different than any other, fresh face from Texas. He had no particular plans other than to check out what the latest cow town had to offer in the way of distraction; the only thing he knew for definite was that he had no desire to return to the Lone Star State where a warrant had been issued for his arrest on at least five counts of murder.

Wild Bill had been informed that the young Texan was in town, but didn't much care. Hickok had a dislike of Texas in general and Texan authorities in particular and would never go out of his way to assist its law enforcement; even now that he wore a marshal's badge himself.

"Take those pistols off, or I'll arrest you." The voice came from behind the young man, "No guns in the city limits."

The town's first marshal, and Hickok's immediate predecessor, Tom Smith, had introduced the no-guns ruling and come up with the novel strategy of persuading the local saloonkeepers and hotel owners into helping enforce it by having them hold on to their patrons firearms for them. It saved the marshal having to confront quite so many armed men, and for the saloonkeepers it meant that many a drinking cowboy would stay and drink not wanting to stray far from his guns. It was a system that everyone seemed to agree to.

"All right, ah don't want any trouble." The Texan turned to find himself face to face with the marshal. Slowly he reached for his pistols and drew them out of the holsters. As the barrels cleared the leather, the young man spun his guns, so that the muzzle faced the law-man, and took a step back to put some distance between them. "Put up your own pistols you long haired scoundrel. I don't hold with those who plan to shoot a boy in the back."

"You've been misinformed," Hickok replied. "I don't do that."

"I know who you are, Hickok, you're a man-killer, and I'll fight the first man that draws a gun on me."

"Kid, you're the gamest and quickest boy I ever saw. Let's compromise on this matter, and I'll be your friend." With that the marshal returned his own Colts to their usual resting place under his tail coat. "Let's head in there," he indicated the door of the nearby American Hotel. "I'll stand you a drink and give you some advice."

The young cowboy smiled as he passed his guns to the lawman. "Sounds like a reasonable plan to me."

The two crossed the threshold of the saloon. "So who do I have the pleasure of joining me in a drink?" Hickok asked.

"John Wesley Hardin," the cowboy smiled and held out his hand.

Hickok took the hand and shook it hearty, "Boy, your reputation proceeds you."

That evening the unlikely pair of the marshal and the killer established a firm friendship, on the basis that the lawman would feign ignorance of the outstanding warrants against the young man as long as that same young man would refrain from murdering anyone while he enjoyed the pleasures of Abilene.

It didn't take Hardin too long to discover the delights of the Bull's Head Tavern and the company of his fellow Texan, Ben Thompson.

"Ya'll know that Hickok hates all Texans." Thompson's familiar refrain was wearing thin with Hardin after several weeks of the same lament.

"So you've said," Hardin pushed his drink across the table waiting for the saloon owner to refill it. It was clear that Thompson wanted something from the gunman; he just hadn't come out and said it yet.

"He'd soon as but a bullet in our backs, as suffer our company."

"He ain't done no harm by me," Hardin responded. "He had the drop on me, could have plugged me in the back." We waved the glass at Thompson again, who eventually poured another shot of rot-gut whiskey. "But he didn't."

"He was sacred of you, John. Knew who you were."

"That don't make no sense, Ben." Hardin shook his head, "If we was scared of me he'd have shot me down than risk a fight."

"He ain't no fighter. That reputation of his is all blow."

"So why not take him yourself then?"

"I'm a respectable business man in this town. me an' Phil Coe have a good thing going here with this establishment. A haven for all the Texas boys at the end of a drive. Except that long-haired perfumed dandy just keeps on gettin' in the way."

"What's your beef with him anyhow?"

"He aims to put us out of business, doesn't like that fact that we draw the cowboys away from the Alamo and the tables there so he can skin them of their money."

"That just seems like business to me. Competition and all that. There's plenty of saloons here in town, what makes you think he's a pickin' on ya'll?"

"He uses his position as the lawman agin' us. Desecrated our sign on the side of the saloon by paintin' it over. Said that certain citizens thought the Bull was a little too anatomically correct. That mural was the first thing the boys ridin' in to town saw. They knew that they had a stoppin' place that understood them with that sign. Without it they just started riding by."

"If you need bull's balls to get men into your saloon, Ben. Then you've got bigger problems than Will Bill." Hardin laughed at his own observation.

"That's just one example." Ben Thompson put his hand flat over the top of Hardin's whiskey glass stopping the gunman from taking another drink.

"Move your hand, Ben." Hardin scowled, "I ain't tellin' ya twice."

The hand stayed. Thompson lowered his voice. "I have a proposition. You get rid of Hickok for me, and I use my influence in Austin to get rid of that pesky warrant hanging over your head."

Hardin pushed the hand off his glass, picked it up and drained the remaining liquid in a single gulp. "You ain't got that sort of pull down south." He fixed Thompson with a stare, "I'm not doing anybody's fighting just now except my own." He placed the glass carefully back on the table. "But I know how to stick to a friend, and Hickok's been a friend since I got to town." John Wesley Hardin stood and pushed his chair back from the table. Looking down at Ben Thompson he added, "If Bill needs killin', why don't you kill him yourself?"

It was a shot that echoed from the upper floor of the American Hotel a month later that broke the truce between the lawman and the outlaw. Hickok heard it as he passed on his evening patrol and immediately headed for the hotel entrance. As he rushed across the lobby he shouted at the hotel clerk

"If Bill needs killin', why don't you kill him yourself?"

"Hardin, which room?"

"101" came the response.

Hickok never broke stride, took the steps two at a time, and was soon stood outside the door with a 101 roughly painted on it. He hesitated. There was no noise coming from the room. Cautiously Hickok pushed against the door with the toe of his boot. It swung open. Not locked.

Close to the bed lay the body of a man.

It looked too big to be the young Texan. The room was empty, but the window was pushed up, and the bed sheets thrown back as if in haste. A pair of trousers hung over the end of the bed. Hickok leant over the body and turned him over. Not a face that he recognized. "Guess he was tryin' to make a name for himself, going after Hardin." Hickok mused to himself. "Probably after the bounty." He pushed the body again with his foot, "How did that turn out for you?"

It was two days later that a thirsty bedraggled cowboy without pants came calling at the town jail asking for Hickok. Deputy Williams tracked him down in the Alamo and persuaded the marshal to come hear the man's story.

The man was stood by a small wagon, pulled by an exhausted looking mule. "Happy to meet you marshal," the cowboy said, "I have a message for you. I was out on the trail and was jumped by a young Texan with no pants on. He had this here cart hidden behind some scrub, and bush whacked me as I rode by. Took my pants," he indicated his own trouserless state, "an' my horse at gunpoint." He shrugged.

"You said something about a message." Hickok, trying to supress his amusement, prompted.

"Oh yeah. He said tell Will Bill that John Wesley Hardin sends his love, and that he'll never set foot in Abilene again."

"So who you going to get to do your dirty work for you now, Thompson?" Wild Bill Hickok leaned on the grubby bar of the Bull Tavern. It wasn't a place he enjoyed frequenting, but as city marshal he felt it his duty to get to know the layout and operation of every saloon and watering hole where trouble might erupt, even if the owners of said establishment wanted him dead.

"There's no need to be like that marshal," Thompson pushed a glass of whiskey in Hickok's direction, which was studiously ignored. "I got nuthin' but respect for you."

"That's not the way I hear it."

"We may have our differences on a few things. But you and I, we're the same.

We both know how to handle ourselves."

"Way I hear it, Thompson. You've hung up the irons an' like to think of yourself as a respectable business owner these days. Killer turned bar-keep"

Ben Thompson didn't say a word. He didn't have to. Hickok had his measure.

"What you doing socializing with that dung-heap?" The question came from the co-owner of the Bull's head who had just entered from the street and was making a beeline for the two men at the bar. Phil Coe strode right up to Hickok. "Get out of my saloon."

"Ain't just yours Phil" Hickok's left hand slipped to rest on the top of his pistols, while the right picked up the glass of whiskey and raised it to his lips, took a sip. "Your partner here," he nodded in Thompson's direction, "was kind enough to stand me a drink when I came a callin.'"

"Well I can't stand you being in here. So get out, and next time you'll feel it."

"That a threat, Mr. Coe?"

"I'm just sayin as I'm a good shot. Ah could kill a crow on the wing if I wanted to."

"Did the crow have a pistol?" Hickok laughed. Then his expression changed, "Was he shooting back? Cause if you try anything, I sure as hell will be." The now empty glass of whiskey was returned to the bar. Hickok tipped the brim of his hat in Thompson's direction, "If you're thinking of sending anyone after me, Ben, just make sure it ain't your hot headed partner here."

"Don't you fret marshal," Coe shouted after the retreating back, "I'll find someone with the stones to face you."

"Maybe we don't need one cowboy." Thompson patted his partner on the shoulder and then pointed at a group of freshly arrived Texan cowhands grouped around a faro table. "Let's go make some friends."

The two saloon owners casually wandered up to the group and watched them for several minutes. The cowboys were losing money, a pretty inevitable consequence of counting on the dumb luck it needs to win at faro. One in particular, a large fellow standing a good head taller than his companions, and equally as distinctive in the breadth of his shoulders and chest, was on the verge of doing something stupid. As Thompson and Coe watched the man lost another bet and his hand instinctively swept down to his holsters. The faro dealer blanched in anticipation, but then smiled. Of course the cowboy's holsters were empty, his colts residing behind the bar as per the marshal's orders. "What you smiling at?" growled the cowboy at the dealer, "if I was carryin' you'd be a dead man. You're a cheat and a thief."

"How much you lose, my friend?" Thompson asked from behind the man's back.

The cowboy wheeled around, "I ain't your friend, and it ain't none of your business." Then he realized who'd spoken to him. "Sorry Mr. Thompson, ah didn't ken it was you."

"So you thinkthe house is cheating on you?"

"No sir, well at least I don't think you is, sire." He gestured back over his shoulder. "But yonder dealer, I ain't so sure about."

"Let me buy you a drink, and see what we can do."

"That's mighty fine you, Mr. Thompson"

"It's Ben. And what do I call you cowboy?"

"Sam," he stuck out a grubby heavily calloused hand. "Sam Hall."

Ben Thompson took the hand and shook it. "Well Sam, how do you feel about our city marshal tellin' us to take your irons away."

"Ah don't like it none. I feel half naked without 'em. But I guess if I want to drink and enjoy myself here I need to do what that damn Yankee scout says."

"So you're okay taking orders from a Yankee lawman?"

"Hell no. In fact if I had my way…." his voice trailed off.

"Let me stand the rest of your boys a drink too, while you and I have a private conversation."

"Come on, Mike." Hickok pushed his chair back to balance on the rear two legs, while the top of the back neatly caught on the wainscot rail that ran along the wall of the Alamo behind him. It was a well practiced move. "They couldn't be that stupid."

"Look, marshal, all I'm doing is passing on what I heard from the barman at the Bull."

"And you're takin' that as gospel."

"He's usually a pretty good source of what goes on there. Thompson and Coe may pay his wages, but he ain't exactly a member of their cheering squad if you get my meaning."

"And he said they'd be here this morning?"

"Yep." Deputy Mike William looked up at the clock on the wall of the Alamo bar. "I'd say you better get heeled if you're gonna do anything about it."

Hickok tipped the chair forward so it landed back on its four feet, leaned down under the card table and picked up a Winchester rifle from where it had been placed on the floor.

"That's new." Williams remarked.

"I've been thinking of trying her out." Hickok smiled. "Maybe today's the day she gets to make her debut."

There was a sudden commotion behind William's back. Hickok leaned to one side to get a look at the cause, as Williams turned to see the part-time jailer John Conkie making his way towards them, pushing card tables and chairs aside in his haste. He was almost out of breath by the time he reached Mike Williams' side. "They're here. Ridin' into town liked they owned the place. All of them are heeled."

"How many?" Williams asked.

"About twenty I reckon. All Texan cowboys as far as I could tell," Conkie responded and then looked straight at Hickok. "They're a comin' for you marshal. The big fellah in front was shouting that they was gonna hang the damn Yankee lawman from the tallest tree on the main street."

Hickok stood, picked up his hat from the table, and headed for the door, carrying his new Winchester repeating rifle instead of his usual shot gun. "Where they at now?" he called back to Conkie.

"Just leavin' The Bull and headed this way."

"Guess I'll go say hello. Seems the friendly thing to do."

Hickok took his usual position on the middle of the street about halfway along the route between the Alamo and The Bull. He smiled to himself when he realized he had decided to make his point outside The Last Chance saloon. It seemed somehow appropriate. It didn't take long before he heard the noise of hoof beats and voices. The posse of riled up angry Texans rounded the corner. Hickok surmised that they had probably been oiled up at The Bull even though it was mid-morning. Thompson and Coe wouldn't have any misgivings about supplying a little dutch courage for those about to do their dirty work for them.

The horsemen pulled up, surprised to see the object of their hunt standing waiting for them. He was outnumbered twenty to one, yet there he was, as bold as brass. Sam Hall pushed the brim of his hat up and glared at the marshal.

"You're makin' it too easy, Hickok."

There was no response.

Hall nudged his horse with his spurs making it take a step or two forward.

"Hold it right there," Hickok called. He raised his Winchester at Hall and then swung it gently to cover the men either side. He had the front echelon of cowboys covered. "Now go ride out, you sons of bitches."

"We ain't riding nowhere Yankee." The response came from somewhere in the pack of cowboys. Hickok couldn't see who had thrown the taunt out. But the big man, who was front and center stood up on his strips, turned, and muttered some obscenity in the direction of the caller.

"My apologies, marshal," he said. "We still aim to be hanging you, but I don't take no disrespect."

"What's your name, Tex?" Hickok replied.

"Sam Hall." The big Texan nodded his head slightly in greeting. The laughed.

"Well now the pleasantries are over with, maybe we can get on with stringing you up."

"No gonna happen." Hickok smiled back.

"There are twenty of us." Hall waved his arm from side to side, then he pulled his colt from his holster and pointed it directly at Hickok. "And just one of you."

During the exchange Hickok had kept sweeping the Winchester across the front row of cowboys, now he lined it up directly at Hall, as if challenging the colt in a head-to-head match off.

"I know what you're thinkin' Hall. Even if I unload all my shells from this here rifle, and my six shooters, you all have way more, and that something is bound to find the mark. I'm a dead man."

Hall nodded but didn't say anything.

"But think again," Hickok said. "If things get to firing, where do you think my first shots are gonna go before you gun me down?" He slowly swung the rifle from side to side again, just to make sure that every member of the hanging party mounted in the front row got time to think about the answer to that question. The rifle. ended pointing back at Hall.

"If you haven't seen one of these before. This here is a Winchester repeating rifle. It holds sixteen shots. I reckon I could get off a good half dozen of those before any of you hit me."

No one said anything.

Time passed. It was probably only a minute, but to Hickok it seemed to last a lot longer. He could see Hall and the other men sitting out front running the possibilities through their minds. Alcohol fueled or not, the logic of a life or death decision was a compelling reason to take a moment to think.

Then one of the riders on the flank turned his horse away and rode back down the street, turned the corner and headed out of town. Two more from the other flank followed. Then four from the rear of the posse followed suite. Gradually the group of twenty angry Texans dwindled away. Only Sam Hall remained. Slowly he replaced the colt in its holster and shrugged his shoulders. "I got to hand it to you marshal, that was the guttiest play I've ever seen." He wheeled his horse around.

"If you're stopping off at The Bull on your way out of town, tell Thompson and Coe it didn't work this time either. And don't forget to hand those irons over to the barman for safe keeping."

"Damn you Hickok,"the big cowboy laughed. He waved his arm in a final salute before turning the corner and heading out of Abilene.

"No Thompson?" Hickok was once again stood at the bar of The Bull during his rounds, but this time he hadn't been approached by the establishment's co-owner.

"He's gone back to Austin," Phil Coe shrugged. "Something about family. He didn't say what."

"When do you expect him back?"

"Can't say, cause he didn't say. You want him for anything special?"

"Just a little reminder that it's been a month or so since you sicced those cowboys on me, and there's been a few old faces I recognize passing through town recently too. Folks I wouldn't exactly call old friends of mine. But you knew that. None of them has the courage to follow up on what ever it is you've been promising them."

"I have no idea what you're talking about," Coe smiled.

"I'm sure you don't."

"You stayin' for a drink, marshal."

"I think I'll pass." Hickok made for the door. As he pushed the swing doors open, he muttered to himself, "I got better places to be."

The marshal always enjoyed his supper at the Kent's house. It was a close to home and what could pass as a normal life these days. He may not admit it but he missed the family back in Illinois. The singular supper invitation following the foiling of the incompetent attempted robbery at the Kent's general store all those months ago had become a habit. Hickok enjoyed his time with the Kent family and his Thursday evening supper visits had become a highlight of his week.

On this particular Thursday, the first in October, he'd been aware of a rising murmur of noise and shouts drifting in from the nearby streets, but had ignored them as much as he could to focus on the family. But it was clear that they too were being distracted as the cause of the noise was clearly getting closer. Eventually the marshal popped the last piece of Mrs. Kent's excellent cornbread in his mouth, dapped the crumbs away from his mustache with the napkin and rose from the table.

"Excuse me, ma'am," he nodded in the direction of his hostess. "I need to see what is causing such a din and interrupting my supper."

"I'll join you," Mr. Kent offered.

The two men stepped out onto the Kent family home porch to see that the street was crowded with a mix of cowboys and townsfolk, who seemed to be enjoying each others company, singing, and making general merriment, as they progressed between a couple of the nearby saloons. Hickok had always stayed wary of the cowboys, it didn't take them long to burn through what little money they made from riding the trail, and they were generally quick to exhibit what Hickok like to refer to as six-gun courage.

Hickok spotted John Conkie, among the throng. "Hey John, what's the celebration for?" Hickok asked.

"Ain't nothin but a bunch of boys havin' a good time before they head home to Texas" Conkie answered with a wave of the bottle that was in his right hand. "Come join us, the cowboys are buying."

Hickok scanned the crowd. "Any guns?"

"Nope," Conkie answered. "They all know the city code."

Hickok stepped down from the porch and approached the cowboy who had his arm linked around Conkie's "Where you boys headed next?"

"The Novelty," he responded in a mix of Texan drawl and alcohol fueled slur.

Hickok pushed his coat back, and the cowboy stiffened in response, but the marshal's hands went past his guns and into a waistcoat pocket. He pulled out a few bills, and pressed them into the cowboy's grimy hand. "Here, you boys have been well behaved since you arrived in town and deserve a last night of fun. Buy your friends a round at the Novelty on me." Hickok turned and returned to the porch, "I hope that Mrs. Kent has some of her excellent apple cobbler on offer this evening."

"I think she might," Kent said as they returned to their interrupted supper.

The knock on the Kent's door came about an hour later. "Well I guess that's my deputy come to get me." Hickok sighed, and pushed back his chair. "It's been a pleasure, as always."

In the background Brian Kent had opened the door to permit Mike Williams into the house.

"Evenin' Mike." Hickok greeted his friend as he pulled on his coat and hat. "I thought you was headin' to Kansas City to check in on family?"

"Evenin' Marshal," Mike grinned, he only ever used Hickok's title at the start of their evening rounds, it had become a little ceremony between the two as if to make the transition form citizen to law officer and official event each day, although to be accurate there were law officers twenty-four hours a day. "Catchin' the train in the morning. Where you want to start this evening?"

"I'm thinking we should check out the Novelty Theater first and see how those cowboys spent my money."

Williams gave him a quizzical look.

"I'll explain on the way over there." Hickok said.

When they arrived at the aforementioned loosely named Theater none of the celebratory cowboys or their press-ganged citizens were to be found.

"Where you boys headed?"

Hickok was stood at the bar talking to the proprietor about the cowboys proposed itinerary when the echoes of a shot reached his ears.

Mike Williams leant in to the doorways from the sidewalk outside, "A shot. Sounded like it came from the Cedar Street direction, Bill."

"I heard it, Mike. Guess we know where the party moved to, except that none of those boys were heeled last I saw them. Stay here in case anyone returns, I'm going to check things out."

"You sure that's a good idea, Bill. What if there's a crowd up there."

"I'm sure I can handle 'em." Hickok patted Williams on the arm as he walked past him back out into the street. Talking up his position in the middle of the road Hickok started off in the direction of Cedar Street he called back, "I'll just see what's going on, then I'll be back."

The cowboys were indeed congregating in Cedar Street but the sense of fun and frivolity had dissipated. Their attention seemed focused on something happening right in front of the Alamo. Hickok pushed his way through the crowd until it opened up into a space in front of the saloon. Stood in the center of the clearing was the only owner of the rival Bull's Head tavern left in town, Phil Coe. Coe looked drunk and angry, and a gun has held loosely in his right hand.

"Put the gun down, Coe." Hickok's voice cut across the murmur of the crowd, "you know the ruling as well as anyone. No guns in town."

Coe smiled and waved the gun around with no thought of where it was pointed. "I meant no harm Marshal, I was after a dog that was theivin' from my kitchens. Chased him up here, an' shot him. All's good."

Hickok looked around, but no deceased canine was in sight. "Anyone see this dog?"

Silence from the crowd.

"No one? Someone go look down the alley." He pointed at the alley that ran along the side of the Alamo saloon.

"Ain't nuthin' in there," the voice belonged to one of the bar-men from the Alamo.

"He's lyin'!" Coe shouted and continued to wave the gun around.

"I believe him, more than you, Coe," Hickok said. "I don't know why you came up here, spoiling the cowboys going away party, but if you just calm down and head back to the Bull's Head I'll forget the violation of the town statute. Go home Phil." Hickok waved a dismissive hand and turned to walk away, intending to leave the cowboys and rejoin his deputy.

"You don't get to call me Phil!" Coe screamed, the gun suddenly clasped firmly in his hand and now pointed at Hickok's back. The click as the hammers were pulled back was unmistakable.

As soon as he'd heard the noise, Hickok spun round and in a single smooth move turned, drew, and fired his twin colts. Coe was hit squarely in the stomach, and as he fell he fired a couple of shots in return. One shot went wide, the other tore through the flap of Hickok's coat, but Hickok was only aware that fire had been returned. Was Coe alone, or was it part of a trap?

As he'd fired he'd caught sight of another figure in his peripheral vision, coming up from behind with pistols drawn. He wheeled and fired two more shots. The man to his left fell and was dead before he hit the floor.

Hickok walked over to were Coe was writhing on the floor, the man was insensible, the wounds fatal. He was gut shot. He was a dead man, maybe not today, maybe not tomorrow, but he was dead.

"If any of you want the rest of these pills, come and get them!' Hickok snarled at the crowd the told the remaining cowboys "Now every one of you mount your horses and ride for camp damn quick." They complied.

"Marshal!"

The cry came from behind, and Hickok turned to see a knot of men stood staring down at the body of the second man, "I think you better get over here." Hickok stepped away from Coe and headed over to the body. As he drew closer he began to realize what he'd done.

Wild Bill Hickok only killed those who deserved to die, it was his central tenant, it was what allowed him to do what he did. He was an avenger and protector of the innocent. That was now shattered. He leant over the body and looked into the face of his Deputy and friend, Mike Williams.

William's hadn't stayed at the Novelty. He'd become concerned about the amount of time Hickok had been gone. He decided the Marshal needed back-up. He'd rushed up to the crowd, guns-drawn and just stepped into the edge of the gun-slinger's vision as the first shots were fired. It was a fatal mistake.

James Buttler Hickok picked up his friend's body and in silence carried him into the nearby Alamo, where he laid him put on the largest poker table in the joint. A location that had often been the site of many of Hickok's greatest personal victories was now a memorial to his greatest personal defeat. Still in silence the marshal reloaded his pistols, checked his shotgun, rearranged the fall of his frock coat, straightened his hat, and stepped out of the Alamo and back into the crisp autumn night.

"It took him four long days to die, ma'am," Ben Thompson, waved the letter in his trembling hand, and that bastard Hickok didn't go see him once. He's never shown a shred of remorse." The letter slid to the floor, the former saloon keeper no longer able to grip it.

"Now Ben, don't go fretting your self over it." The old lady smiled a cold smile. There was no sadness in her eyes at the thought of her lost son, only the steely stare of revenge. "Y'all got enough to worry about gettin' over your hurtin.'"

"I shouldn't be stuck here in Texas. The crazy buggy accident didn't kill me, but it may as well have for all the use I am down here."

"Don't you go cussin' Texas, Ben."

"Ah didn't mean no disrespect Ma Coe."

"Good." The old lady rose from her seat, bent over and picked the letter up from the floor. "I'll see to that dandy Hickok."

"It's from Mr.Hickok, ma'am," the cable office messenger boy had run from his post at the Kansas City railroad station. He was hot an out of breath, but he felt this was a note that needed to be delivered personally.

The lady of the house accepted the note with a graceful sniffle and gave the boy a couple of coins for his trouble. He face was red from tears, her dress a mourning black.

"Any response, ma'am?"

The lady read the note. "He's wired me the money to go fetch my boy." She sniffed again, then pulled herself together. "No response, but book me a ticket for the next train to Abilene. It's time to bring my boy home."

"Sure thing Mrs. Williams."

Hickok saw them get off the train. All three of them. They tried to make it look like they weren't traveling together. They'd alighted from different cars, but the clothes marked them out as Texas boys, and they were new at this, as they all glanced at each other in conformation of their arrival. Hickok ignored them and let them pass him on their way into town. He was here for a different reason.

When he saw the black mourning clothes, made dusty from the journey, the feelings of guilt rose again. Mike Williams hadn't needed to die, and especially not at his hands. No-one could notice it from his behavior, he still did his rounds, still acted the same, still treated people the same, but James Butler Hickok was a changed man. Something inside had broken, if it came to another fight would he be so sure of himself as he had been? Would he hesitate, would he harm another innocent? He didn't know the answers but the questions gnawed at him night and day.

Hickok stepped forward and helped the frail form of Mrs Williams down from the carriage steps and towards a buggy.

"I'd like to go see Micheal, please Mr. Hickok."

Michael. He'd never heard William referred to by his full name. It didn't sound right, yet when she said it; it was full of pride, love, and sorrow.

"Mrs. Williams…" he started to speak, and found he couldn't. Was he about to apologize, to explain? He didn't know, his mind just shut down, unable to find the right words to utter.

"It's fine Marshal. No recriminations. He was doing his job, alongside a man he admired."

Damn, that hurt even more. Hickok stayed quiet and helped her into the buggy. "The funeral parlor" he told the driver, and watched it drive away down the dusty street of Abilene. Watching it go, Hickok walked off in the other direction, to the Alamo.

The expanse of his usual table at the Alamo seemed wider these days. No-one sat with him. No-one dared to play in case a sudden movement or a misspoken word would prompt those reflexes. Hickok may have kept the fact that he no longer trusted himself a personal matter, but the truth was that he was no longer trusted by those he protected. If he gunned down his right-hand man, who else may be caught by those guns. Hickok just sat and stared at the whiskey sitting on the table before him. A cough caught his attention. He looked up to find John Conkie stood in front of him across the table.

"What can I do for you, John?"

"Bill there's word goin' around that three Texans are gunnin' for you."

"I saw them arrive." He picked up the whiskey at last and downed it in a single gulp, letting the liquid burn his mouth and warm his gullet on the way down. "They'll be like all the others. All talk and no action."

"Ah don't think so. Not this time. Word is that Coe's mother has raised a bounty of ten thousand on you." Conkie pulled out the chair nearest to him and sat down. He stared straight at his friend, and keeping his voice low intoned, "There's goin' be shootin' Bill. They mean business."

"No." Hickok's voice was equally low, but held a note of finality. "No more shooting, no more innocents are going to die 'cause of me."

Conkie was surprised, it was the only acknowledgement he heard from the marshal about the events on Cedar Street. "What's your plan?"

"I don't have a plan. I just know that this is over an it's time to move on." Hickok's hand moved from the empty glass he'd been nursing up to his vest. With a slight tug that left a small rent in the fabric he pulled the city marshal's badge away, laid it on the table, and after a few seconds slid it across to the city jailer. "Take this, find another marshal. My time in Abilene is done. Mrs. Williams will be taking Mike's body back home to Kansas City tomorrow. I'll be on that train too."

⁂

Hickok had never felt comfortable traveling in trains. It didn't matter which way you faced on those bench seats it was impossible to keep an eye on both doors at either end of the carriage. Luckily the train wasn't crowded and Mrs. Williams wanted to sit by herself in her grief. Hickok was fine with that, even though he as paying her expenses he didn't want her to feel any obligation, nor did he expect any civility or friendship on her behalf, he had killed her son after all.

So he took the seat across the aisle, and sat sideways with his back pressed against the window, with one leg stretched out on the seat to discourage anyone who may have the fleeting thought of joining him. From this position he could alternate his focus between the carriage doors. It still wasn't enough, as he was looking right one of the Texan's appeared in the cabin from the left. Hickok caught the movement in the corner of his eye, but recent events served as a momentary brake on his actions.

The click of the gun's hammer being drawn back echoed around the carriage. Mrs. Williams gasped.

"Ah, got you now, Hickok," the Texan drawled. "I'm gonna be the man who killed Wild Bill." He giggled to himself.

"Not here," Hickok said, his voice flat. "Not in front of a woman already grieving. She don't need to see this."

The giggler paused and looked at Mrs. Williams. He seemed to consider Hickok request for a second or two. "OK, Marshal. This way." He waved his gun back in the direction from which he'd come.

Hickok could see the outline of the other two Texans waiting on the platform between the carriages. "I ain't a marshal no more."

"Don't make no difference to me. My brother there," he again waved his gun towards the end of the carriage. "Did have a couple of doubts about killin' a lawman. But guess he ain't got anything to worry about now." He giggled again. "He'll be happy to hear it. Now git going."

The giggler followed Hickok onto the swaying platform. He was boxed in by the three of them, he had nowhere to go, and no room to maneuver. But neither did they. Nor could they shoot him here as there was a chance they'd hit each other.

"Good day, gents." Hickok addressed the other two waiting men. "So what's our play?" As he spoke the train went over a sidings point on the track, a branch line to who knew where. But it was Hickok's salvation for the carriages swayed a little more violently than usual. The giggler behind lost his footing and lurched at Hickok for stability. Instinctively trying to grab on to something for balance he dropped the gun he'd had leveled at Hickok. Will Bill kicked it off the edge of the platform, and continued the movement to draw his boot and spurs down the shin of the falling man, who collapsed in a heap on floor. The other two Texans took their eyes off the prize and stepped forward to help their downed colleague. Hickok took his chance and delivered a straight arm punch into the chest of the nearest bounty hunter, who was pushed back into the third. The two staggered back. Off the edge of the platform and disappeared under the wheels of the following carriage.

"Travis," the giggler shouted, presumably the name of his recently departed brother. Hickok looked down at the crumpled figure on the floor before him, drew his colts, and fired. Yep, he only killed those that deserved killing.

He kicked the body off the platform, and without a word returned to his seat.

It wasn't the Alamo, hell it wasn't even the Bull's Head. But it was a saloon with a poker game, and that was all that James Butler Hickok needed from Kansas City at this particular moment. As usual he was sat with his back to the wall, keeping the door in sight, just in case.

"You playing, or day dreaming?" The young cow hand to his left growled.

"Leave him be," the older hand further round the table said. "He came in from Abilene, and I hear they're burying that deputy who got murdered today."

"You know him." The young player asked.

Hickok just stared at the boy, who shifted uncomfortably in his seat. "Just deal." The cards were dealt and Hickok picked up the latest card to add to the fan in his hand. The nine of diamonds.

THE END

MUSINGS ON WILD BILL
Part Two - Endings

The two stories of mine in this volume are intended to bookend Wild Bill Hickok's career as a gunfighter. *Wild Duck* recounted his first gunfight, while *Alamo Reflex* told the story of the last. Like its predecessor it is largely based on recorded facts, with a few authorial embellishments along the way.

By the time of the events recounted in *Alamo Reflex,* both Hickok's fictional legend, and factual reputation, were well known. In many ways he was one of the frontier's first celebrities. And he was more than happy to make the most of it. The events in Abilene would change that.

They say that one of the pitfalls of writing historical fiction is knowing more about your characters fate than they do, and that you should avoid any foreshadowing that points to what should be an unknown future. Well, rules are meant to be broken. The hand of cards at the beginning, two aces, two eights, nine of diamonds is now known as the Dead Man's Hand. An allusion to the fact that this is the hand of cards Wild Bill Hickok was holding when he was shot and killed during his time in Deadwood many years after this story is set. It maybe a little bit of on-the-nose foreshadowing, but I enjoyed throwing it in.

Following the siege and battle the name of the Alamo became a touchstone across the west. The saloon in Abilene was far from the only one to co-opt it, especially in the towns along the cattle drive routes from Texas. Despite his aversion to the Lone Star State, this particular Alamo was Hickok's favorite haunt even during his time as marshal spending more time at its tables than in his city supplied office. The layout of the extensive saloon outlined here is based on contemporary descriptions. As is Hickok's description and clothing. He certainly cut a dashing figure, and his well documented habit of bathing each day was unusual for the time.

The Kent family (A nod to my in-laws. I hope they appreciate the name check.) and their mercantile store are my invention, but there is a report of a similar event where Hickok foiled a robbery just because of his reputation.

Despite my research reading I never got a handle on what exactly his problem with Texas was. But it seems that there was one Texan he did get along with, fellow man-killer John Wesley Hardin. Hickok's encounter with the young Hardin was in Hardin's autobiography and it seemed the two retained an ongoing respect for each other's reputation even if their paths never crossed again. However the Texas angle certainly fueled the feud between Hickok and the owners of the Bull Tavern. The reasons for the Ben Thompson and Phil Coe's argument with Hickok are as outlined here, A matter of state pride, competitive interests in different salons, hurt pride, and just downright antagonism on both sides. Of the two Ben Thomson had the greater reputation as a fighter and killer, he was probably the closest that Hickok had to a true rival at the time. However they never had the opportunity to put that theory to the test. Thompson's absence from Abilene at the climax due to being injured in a buggy accident while visiting Texas is a fact.

Phil Coe on the other hand seems to have been more bluster than skill. He seemed to prefer shooting off his mouth to shooting his guns. Hickok's come back to Coe about the crow shooting back is reported dialog from an encounter between the two. Where possible I've tried to insert snatches of several other exchanges.

The other Texan in the story, cowboy Sam Hall, is fictitious, but the encounter with a gang of Texas cowboys outside the Last Chance saloon actually happened. As did Hickok facing off against them on his own just armed with Winchester repeating rifle. Although in truth they were on foot rather than on horseback as I have them. Having the hero face down a gang on horseback just seemed more visually appealing.

With the exception of starting out at the fictitious Kent house, the events surrounding the death of Mike Williams are pretty much as outlined in the enquiry into the shooting. Although there does seem to be disagreement as to whether Williams was due to head back to Kansas City that night to see either his wife, or his mother. I went with the mother as it seemed to make the tragedy that more poignant. Hickok was reportedly devastated by killing not only an innocent man, but a close friend as well. It broke his spirit as a gun-fighter, and according to some sources this was the last time he fired a gun in anger.

Phil Coe's mother did put out a sizable reward for Hickok's death, but only the three Texans who followed him on to the train seemed to have shown any interest in attempting to follow through. The fight on the train is fictitious, in reality the three men left Hickok alone, and whole revenge bounty thing seems to have been forgotten.

In an interesting parallel to the post-shootout events at Rock Creek years earlier, Hickok once again tried to make restitution through cash. This time he paid for William's body to be returned to Kansas City and for his funeral, which Hickok didn't attend.

No one knows where he was at the time of the funeral, he may have stayed in town, and he may have played another game of poker to take his mind off things. Wherever he was it was the start of the journey that would take him to Deadwood and that fateful hand of cards.

ALAN J. PORTER - Writer, and award-winning editor, Alan J. Porter, has written adventures featuring Sherlock Holmes, Allan Quatermain, Houdini, and private eye Rick Ruby; as well as his own New Pulp adventurers, The Raven and The Lotus Ronin.His pop-culture non-fiction work has featured properties such as Batman, Star Trek, The Beatles, and James Bond. He has also written comics for Tokyopop, BOOM Studios, Marvel, Disney, and Kid Domino.

WYATT EARP

"A World Aflame"

by George Tackes

Wyatt Earp clutched the human trash by the scruff of his neck and the seat of his pants. Earp heaved the drunken buffoon down the short hallway, through the oaken exterior door, and out into the dirt roadway. From the gas lighting behind the brothel's stoop, he eyeballed a gray cloud of dry grit surround the sloppy lush.

"And don't come back, Twaddler," Earp growled as he clapped his hands together to scatter the grime from them. "At least, not until you've sobered up some."

"Damn you, Blackie," the drunken Twaddler slurred as he rubbed his bald pate.

No one called Wyatt Earp, Wyatt Earp here in this small Illinois town. It was just what he wanted. The way it had to be.

Everyone in Urbana knew the bouncer as John Black, but called him "Blackie." Some called him that because of the ebony color of his hair and moustache. Some because of his perpetually dark mood.

"You can't grope our girls from behind and say that you're a human corset, Twaddler."

Twaddler grinned, wiggled his graying walrus moustache, and giggled. Then, he crawled to the edge of Market Street and passed out.

Earp spun around on his heel and strode back inside the brothel with a strained smile on his face. He thought the human corset joke was kind of funny. But it was his job to keep order in this whorehouse.

The twenty-three-year-old Earp had little in common with the forty-seven-year-old Edmund Twaddler. However, both were bitter about losing their wives and drank about it most of the time. In fact, they jointly drank themselves into a stupor on more than one occasion at the whorehouse.

"Did you throw out the little bum on his ear, Blackie?" asked Madame Jane, the red-headed, gaudily dressed proprietor of the Boneyard Creek Social Club.

Earp just nodded.

Just over Urbana's corporate northeastern limits, the two-story stone Italianate bordello with its slightly sloped roof and extended eaves, each supported by a hand-carved ornamental bracket, was neither an exclusive nor a secret club. It boasted a game room, full-length bar, lushly-furnished parlor, and small ballroom, with eight bedrooms for entertainment upstairs.

The Boneyard Creek Social Club, typically slow for a Sunday night, catered to any man with enough money to be pleasured. Some men openly patronized the establishment, but most preferred discretion.

Earp understood the difference, but didn't care.

He'd toss any one of them on their ass if they "misbehaved." His Army-issue

Colt was obviously tucked in his back of his pants' belt. He didn't want to use it, and, at six feet tall, he didn't need to. But he wouldn't hesitate to pull it out and threaten anyone, if the need arose.

He resumed his corner post with the widest viewpoint of the clients and ladies. He glanced out the tall, rounded window at the stream from which the brothel took its name and the blackened, dried out woods beyond. The dark water barely flowed in the branch of the Vermillion River. It had been a long, dry summer into this first week of October. So little rain fell that the Boneyard Creek was a trifle more than a shallow brook. The acres of dry timber along it were cracked and brittle and starved for moisture.

Earp heard the homespun superstitious folklore about the origin of the name "Boneyard". Legend had it that local Indians, mostly Potawatomi and Kickapoo, hung their dead over the creek, allowing the bones to fall into it. He knew that many Native American peoples removed the flesh and organs from bones before burial. Supposedly, the tributary was full of bones when the first settlers arrived except no person or document confirmed that human bones were actually found in excavations along the tributary.

And he wasn't sure if those local tribes practiced excarnation anyway.

A ruckus drew his attention back inside to the parlor. Blackie broke up a drunken brawl. Two reporters, one from the Champaign County Gazette and the other from the Urbana Republican, threw punches at each other. Most jabs missed and the ones that landed were little more than a strong nudge. He sent each reporter away with an experienced lady of the evening to separate corners.

Right after that, he gripped a blonde hooker's arm from clobbering a patron from behind. The wet-behind-the-ears patron stupidly commented on the blonde's weight. He shooed the hooker off to entertain another client as he smacked the young fool in the back of the head.

The rest of the evening proceeded as usual. Sex and drinking were the primary activities. Because Earp was an excellent gambler, gambling rarely occurred in that house of ill repute. If he sat in a hand, he was certain to win it.

Throughout the evening, he personally escorted several customers out the door after he made sure their bills were paid in full.

Only once, Earp prevented a potential client from entry. As a rule of thumb, the Boneyard Creek Social Club catered to any man with enough money. Except if he was from Champaign. Champaign residents were highly unwelcome at the Social Club and in Urbana in general.

(The reporter from the Champaign County Gazette worked and lived in town his entire life. In fact, the young sandy-haired native was often referred to as "an old town man.")

Earp politely persuaded the Champaignite to take his business elsewhere. He was well aware of the rivalry with the town to the west and contempt for its residents.

The feud between the two small towns had started seventeen years before when the new town of West Urbana developed around the new train depot for the Chicago branch of the Illinois Central Railroad. Urbana city fathers believed it made sense to have the train depot in their town, the county seat.

However, the Illinois Central executives decided to lay track in the flatter ground two miles west of Urbana.

To add further insult to injury, West Urbana changed its name to Champaign about ten years back.

Earp fancied no opinion either way. He just wanted to keep the peace.

And he kept the peace even after the last customer wandered out the door and the girls were tucked in bed.

Madame Jane finished counting the night's take and gave Earp his cut. A one-time beauty and twice Earp's age, she still occasionally enjoyed the company of men and winked at the young bouncer.

To her, prostitution was a successful business venture. Whatever her upbringing, she never viewed it in terms of morality.

"Always a good night when nothing gets broken. You did a nice job of keeping the girls safe too. How about some personal security for me?" she purred.

He nodded and maintained his scowl. The nod indicated he heard her. The scowl meant that tonight, however, they wouldn't be sharing a bed together.

After work, he headed home in the dark. Unlike most townspeople, he didn't own a horse. A horse would attract unwanted attention and unneeded expenses. He sold his after arriving and could buy one in a moment's notice. Brenner, a livery owner, owed him a favor in that regard.

So he trudged over the uneven, dirt road of Market Street. He crossed the Illinois, Bloomington, and Wabash tracks west into downtown Urbana. His boots clomped and scraped along the baked, planked sidewalks along Main Street.

In the silent early morning, he strolled on the south side of the dusty boulevard. He glanced in the darkened windows of a harness shop, tobacconist, general store, and bakery.

Earp paused at the Tiernan Brothers' nearly completed three-story brick opera house. Directly across from the street was the Busey Brothers' year-old two-story brick opera house. This made the dour man chuckle out loud. The outrageous rivalries in this town actually made him laugh.

Turning south on Race Street, Earp sucked in the warm, clear air and headed to his rented house a block south. Instead of walking along the road, he ambled through the oaks and sycamores and elms toward the two-room solitary cottage.

This allowed him privacy that a less-expensive rooming house would not. Nobody would pry into his business and, if he wanted to spend the day drunk, no one would object.

Essentially, he favored the wide open spaces that Urbana offered him. Except for its downtown, Urbana's comprehensive layout was uncluttered. Houses weren't on top of one another like in other places he traveled through. Only the downtown was crowded with tall tenements. Otherwise, only one or two single-family homesteads were randomly sprinkled among the lots. Almost every lot accommodated at least one stable with at least one horse residing in each. A wagon or carriage typically stored inside as well. The folks here were the type to unhesitatingly loan him a horse if an emergency arose.

Earp welcomed that emergencies rarely arose here. That was something else he appreciated.

He passed by the small withered house he rented to Green and Race Streets, a block south. Nearly every night, his bitterness compelled him unless he was incredibly drunk.

As his wont when sober, he paused in front of the Methodist Episcopal Church at the corner. Its steeple disappeared into the lightless sky. He was drawn to it like a battered woman to an abusive husband. He bent over and picked up a loose cobblestone laying in one of the dirt roadway's ruts.

Earp stood in the early morning gloom before the church rubbing his thumb against the smooth stone in his hand, deciding which stained glass window to shatter. He hurled it in anger, hoping that small stone would bring the entire structure down like the walls of Jericho. But instead the rock struck a single brown stone and trickled down impotently.

"Damn you," Earp said. This last year ruined his life. He married and became a father. A few months later, he was a widower and childless. Typhoid took them both. Then, he got involved in a bad business deal. He lost money from a public fund and got arrested for the shady dealings connected to the whole bad business. His business partner disappeared with money.

Last June, Earp escaped from a jail in Peoria after being arrested for horse theft. The trial would have proven his innocence but instead, he made his way east. He wound up as a bouncer at various brothels along the way. Plenty of work was always available in that. He was tall and strong and mean. Heaps of brothels were looking for bitter, tough thugs to guard their property – the building, the booze, and the broads. A few weeks ago, he stumbled onto Madame Jane's sublime whorehouse.

Weary and defeated, Earp drifted north back to his rented rooms. He paid on time and in cash, so the Tiernan Brothers, who owned the property, didn't care what he did or whatever his real name may be.

He concluded his trek to bed unimpeded. He'd sleep and wake up and go back to work at the Boneyard Creek Social Club.

As Earp fell asleep, Twaddle opened his eyes. He woke up next to a horse post across the street from the closed Social Club with its shuttered windows.

A tired swayback disturbed his slumber. The dark American Saddlebred was foaming at the mouth. It looked wore out and walked past the drunk at a very slow four-beat rhythm. It needed to be watered and rested.

On it sat a man, a tall, muscular man with limp brown hair and dark moustache. The man was scruffy, sweaty, and used up like the horse.

Light from the Harvest Moonlight allowed Twaddler to watch the tall man with a day's beard growth guide the horse toward the railroad tracks. Through blurred eyes, he saw the rider slump off the horse. He heard the horse stagger over to the creek to drink and fall over.

The horseback rider looked around and spotted Twaddle. He recognized Twaddler as one of the town drunks. He shrugged, smiled, and toppled against the Social Club's outer wall.

Twaddler's nose detected the pungent mixture of human sweat with horse sweat. His ears listened to the man's deep, grumbling snores.

Twaddler similarly began to doze. The dilapidated stable where he slept on occasion was just a few steps away. But he was comfortable in the warm October morn.

Drowsy, he considered his need for spending money. He occasionally helped with the horses at the local liveries. His experience in the U.S. Calvary during the Civil War was more in tending to the horses than riding into battle. He rode very little, but mostly watered and groomed the horses for battle. He saw very little action.

However, Twaddler knew he could make a quick buck from someone who wanted information about any stranger coming into town.

Being one of Urbana's natives, he knew everyone in the region. He did not know who this sleeping man was.

Assured of drinking money, Twaddler nodded off. He lulled himself to sleep with nasty thoughts of Champaign.

Like most native Urbanites who had an opinion about the town to its west, he despised Champaign, Illinois.

His wife ran off a few years ago after he returned from the War. The worst part she left him for some dude in Champaign.

Before the Civil War that town stole a train depot from his town.

That provoked Urbana to one up Champaign by tearing down its County Courthouse and building a grander structure. A source of pride and joy to townies, this assured that Urbana would remain the county seat of Champaign County.

About the same time Twaddler's wife deserted him, Champaign pompously organized a fire department. Urbana didn't need such high-falutin' extravagance. Its volunteer bucket brigade proved its worth over and over.

Then three years earlier, Champaign County was selected as the site for Illinois Industrial University, the new state agricultural school. Mostly it was due to the influence of state legislator Clark Griggs.

Twaddler was still enraged that Griggs, a former mayor of Urbana, arranged it to be shared between both towns instead of just his town.

Several attempts to merge the towns through elections were repeatedly defeated by the intense and persistent rivalry.

Twaddler would be perfectly satisfied if a sink hole magically appeared and sucked Champaign and its entire population to the pits of Hell. Such musing soothed Twaddler back into a peaceful slumber through the rising morning sun.

More than a few hours of sleep later, Earp ate his usual lunch of lamb, potatoes, and coffee with a bit of whiskey added at The Main Street Café.

The downtown restaurant owned by Shuck and Hollister on Main Street was filled to capacity with its usual Monday crowd. Businessmen gathered for lunchtime deals. A few City Council members with the mayor were in attendance. Earp knew some of the customers professionally, but the mayor was not one of them.

Earp ate in silence betraying no confidences. His focus was an unfamiliar man with a scruffy face. He took in the measure of the man.

The man was more than six feet tall and muscular. Unshaven but rested, the man clearly regularly sported a hazel moustache, but not a beard. His clothes were plain brown and dirty with scuffed boots. Even his white shirt was browned with grit and dried sweat stains. His stringy drab hair clumped together by sweat.

By Hollister's reaction, the man smelled badly. However, money always smelled good to Hollister.

The man quietly ordered his lunch of meat sandwiches and whiskey. He looked grumpy, but with a wicked smile like a secret duty was placed upon him. A mission. A divine mission of sorts.

"Damn you, Snyder!" a sandy haired and bearded man shoved an older man. The same two men who argued the night before at the Social Club.

Snyder didn't get mad but guffawed.

"All's fair in love and newspaper."

"You stole another advertiser!"

"The Republican has a bigger readership than the Gazette."

The rancid stranger like the other patrons couldn't help but stare at the quibbling journalists.

Noticing that they became the center of attention, the sandy-haired man spoke in a lower voice, "Let's take this outside."

The two men scurried outside.

The stranger concentrated on the two as they continued to argue. His red-rimmed eyes never left the front window which framed the men.

Earp was concerned. Not exactly worried, but concerned about the stranger. Strangers in a small town are always suspicious.

But for Earp, he was especially wary. Since Earp escaped from a jail, he'd been on the run since. He worked at one whorehouse after another. Whenever a stranger who looked like a bounty hunter or uncorrupted constable, Earp would disappear and move further east until he finally wound up at Madame Jane's establishment a few weeks ago.

Now, another stranger appeared.

Twaddler plopped down across from Earp, blocking his view of the stranger.

"What do ya want, Twaddler?" he grunted and looked into his coffee.

"I'm hungry, Blackie," Twaddler grinned with yellow stained teeth and bad breath. "And thirsty."

"Hit the road!"

"I'm not beggin'. I got something you may want to know."

"Doubt it."

"I'm willin' to earn my keep, Blackie."

"Hit the road!"

"You want to know about that there stranger over there? Someone no one knows eating and plotting something."

A slight flick of Earp's eyes betrayed him.

Twaddler sat back and beamed with his lips closed.

Hollister waddled over to Earp's table to present the bill and asked, "Want me to take to out the garbage?"

"Nah. Give him what he wants."

"My good sir, I'll have what Blackie's having."

Earp slipped Hollister more than twice the amount of the bill to cover the cost of Twaddler's meal.

Hollister toddled off with an extra spring in his step.

"Whacha got?"

"Well, I saw him ride in this mornin' on a swayback frothing at the mouth. He comes from up north. Chicago to be exact. Bragged about riding all night.

He tol' me when he asked about where to get something to eat. Acted like he was proud of running that horse to death. Southerner from the way he talks."

"Bounty hunter?"

"Didn't say. But definitely not from these parts. Not a sheriff or deputy or some kind of city constable. But something about him, ain't right. Acting like he's on some sort of assignment."

It wasn't worth the price of the meal, but it was something. Besides, Earp knew that he'd make it back from Twaddler later that evening.

The tall man tossed some coins onto the table and strutted out of the Main Street Cafe. Blackie followed.

His work day would begin little more than an hour. He reckoned it should be slow for a Monday night, but one could never be certain. The unusually warm, weather stirred a man's desires, lust.

Tucking a clean napkin under his chin and over his stained shirt, Twaddler tilted back and waited for his first full meal in days.

The tall man in the brown clothes walked with long, decisive steps west on Main Street and down Race Street.

Earp was uneasy because the stranger headed toward the house he was staying at.

The man hiked past it.

Earp still wasn't convinced that the stranger wasn't a bounty hunter. He could still be the reason the man came to Urbana. He kept his distance. Not many people were about on this warm October afternoon.

The man continued to the Methodist church. He looked around and stepped inside the church, empty now, with morning services concluded. A church is a good source of information on locals.

Earp was about to enter the house of worship when a lanky, clean-shaven businessman tapped him on the shoulder. He instantly recognized the serious-looking fellow as Mayor Eli Halberstadt .

As Earp followed the suspected bounty hunter, the mayor must have followed Earp.

"Mr. Black, how are you?" the mayor bellowed with a sincerely hearty greeting.

"Hello, Mr. Mayor."

"Eli, please."

"Eli. Call me 'Blackie,' Eli."

Earp couldn't but help but like the mayor, his third year in office. He never saw the mayor at the Social Club, but the mayor never shunned anyone who visited the establishment either.

"Missed you at services yesterday, Blackie."

"Don't attend."

"Missed you at services yesterday, Blackie."

"You're a Methodist? Or so I heard."

"My kin is."

"You're not?"

"If there's a God, He hasn't dealt me a very obliging hand. So I'd rather like to think there isn't one."

"Dear. Dear. What a pity," the mayor proffered sincerely.

Earp shrugged.

"Well, sir. I daresay you need to see the good that God can place in people," the mayor spoke softly. "If you ever change your mind, please come pray with us."

They shook hands and parted on friendly terms.

Maybe he's campaigning early, Earp thought cynically.

He turned and searched for the scruffy man in the soiled brown clothes. Since he perceived no sign of the man, Earp deduced that he must still be inside. He rushed across the brown lawn, up the cement steps into the church.

Earp scanned across the wooden polished pews toward the pulpit. He spotted the scruffy man. The man hesitated by the log tapered candles beside the pulpit. The congregation was gathering them for the upcoming All Saints Day services, less than a month away.

Earp recalled how Methodists only used candles with actual flames as part of worship service.

The man dashed into the rear room.

Earp retreated out the front door, the way he came in.

He clearly spotted the stranger carrying something under his outer jacket. He couldn't see exactly what it was, but he has his suspicions.

The man bolted south down an alley.

Earp quickly narrowed the distance between them.

When the man curved east at the first alley, Earp was close behind.

The man ducked behind a pair of stables.

Earp recognized the two clapboard back-to-back stables as belonging to the Widow Sheperd and the Widow Whitlock. Bales of hay filled the empty stalls where the tack was stored. The horses and wagons were out earning their keep for the widows.

Earp paused by an open stable door. He hesitated when he detected movement inside the first stable.

Closer inspection revealed a couple little boys trapping cockroaches beside the middle stall. They giggled. One produced a box of matches. The other boy slapped the ground and picked up a plump black cockroach. The other struck a match and fried the bug's thin legs in his friend's fingers. Then, they chuckled as they watched the roach flit around in the dirt by flapping its wings.

Earp didn't know if school was out or if the boys were playing hooky. He had very little to do with children since his infant son died.

Earp smiled along with the boys. He remembered him and his brothers playing that same way in their youth on his father's farm in Monmouth.

He would have remained lost in his youthful reminisces if it wasn't for the palpable gray smoke whirling around in the paddock at the opposite end of Widow Sheperd's stable door. The inviting smell of burning leaves drew him away.

Earp stepped over to Widow Whitcomb's stable.

Instinctively, he grabbed for his gun.

The stranger stood sneering in the middle of flames. A rolled cigarette hung in his sneer as he shoved a long taper candle against a bale of hay. Melted paraffin wax spattered on dry hay. A flicker of a flame trailed from the greasy candle wax.

Earp's mouth gaped open at the speed. His eye followed the flames flow upward like a reverse waterfall and joined the other flames in a lake of fire above his head in the rafters.

It diverted his gaze from the arsonist. The arsonist sidled next door to the other stable.

Earp shifted over to follow him.

The arsonist stood with a revolver, probably a Colt like his, in one hand and the burning candle in the other. He pointed the gun at the two oblivious boys still playfully burning the legs off the disgusting bugs. Without uttering a single word, the man waved his revolver downward.

Earp dropped his gun onto a nearby bale of hay and raised his hands. The dry straw muffled any sound which might have alerted the boys to danger. The mischievous youngsters thought the burning smell and wisps of smoke were due to their high jinks.

The arsonist nodded and tossed his candle into a hay-laden stall. The bundles smoldered and then erupted in a wide orange and yellow blaze. He side stepped to the east out of the alley.

Earp lunged for his weapon and screamed at the boys.

"Get out of here."

The wide-eyed boys jerked their heads up out of their revelry. They now noticed the east side of the stable wall on fire. Scared, they were paralyzed with fear.

Shoving his gun back into his pants, he gripped terrified boys by their shoulders. He jammed his thumbs into their shoulder blades to turn them around and force them away of the fiery stalls.

By the time the trio stepped into the alley, the entire stable was in flames. Moments later, part of the roof collapsed on top of the box of matches they were playing with. The tiny flare from the matchbox barely added to the growing bonfire.

It was two o'clock in the afternoon. They were two square blocks south of Main Street, downtown Urbana.

Earp headed west beside the boys to Race Street. He could clearly see the stone steeple of the Methodist Church and headed toward it.

When he knew they were all clear of danger, Earp breathed a sigh of relief. He realized the arsonist wasn't tracking him for a reward because he ran the other way.

The two boys continued to run north. The entire way they yelled, "Fire! Fire!" as they raised the dust on the road behind them.

By the time, they reached the next street; Mayor Halberstadt organized the volunteer bucket brigade. Experienced men seized large metal pails available from every household and business. For water to extinguish fire, they knew the location of every handy horse trough, well, pump, and rain barrel.

More curious than hungry, Twaddler followed the others townspeople out into the street to see what the ruckus was all about. He joined the spectators at the corner. Men, women, and children formed on the east and west sides and treated this ongoing calamity more of a local sporting event.

Hearing Halberstadt's call to alarm to the onlookers, Twaddler got out of the way of the volunteers. Lacking any fire-fighting know-how, he didn't even think to offer aid. Since his attendance wouldn't be required, his hunger took precedence over his curiosity. He noticed that even Hollister was distracted by the fire and the fire-fighting activities.

On his return to the empty restaurant, the town drunk passed by opportunistic shoplifters helping themselves to pastries, spurs, cigars, watches, canned goods, and various other sundries in downtown Urbana. He meandered into The Main Street Café and helped himself to a slice of apple pie.

A couple of blocks south, two frantic boys directed the forming bucket brigade to where the raging inferno specifically started. Black smoke obscured the exact original location of the fire. Clucking chickens and squealing horses could be heard from every direction. The sharp aroma of charred mahogany and burning leaves filled the autumn air. The afternoon heat intensified to an almost tangible object like boiling molasses.

Prevailing winds from the southwest, comparable to a hurricane, swirled and twisted the choking smoke and disguised the spread of the fire.

Within five minutes, flames hopped to a backyard willow and engulfed Widow Whitcomb's house and outhouse. The trees' remaining leaves provided a direct line from the stable to the home.

The wooden fence separating the properties was aflame from the leaves littered against it.

Widow Sheperd's house was burning as well.

Thanks to the boys' warning, the bucket brigade expertly formed a human chain north of the fire along Green Street. They began dousing the flames containing the conflagration despite the sparks and fiery debris floating over their heads due to the high winds.

Earp ignored the request to join the brigade. He judged that they had things well in hand and he had to go to work.

Three, four, five buckets were poured at a time onto the flames. Then, they handed the empty pails to men behind them. They passed the containers to other men who scooped more water out of troughs and rain barrels or pump them from wells. Filled buckets were again emptied to allow the men to advance on the fire. All under the rhythmic counting of Halberstadt.

"1, 2, 3, pour! 1, 2, 3, pour," he repeated over and over like a coxswain to a rowing crew.

The volunteers kept up with the cadence being shouted at them. No one expected the 51-year-old mayor to lift or toss buckets of water. His job was to oversee the progress and assure success.

"1, 2, 3, pour! Colonel Busey, get some men and create a fire break along Market and Green! "1, 2, 3, pour," Halberstadt ordered.

Fifteen years younger than Halberstadt , Councilman Samuel T. Busey, "The Hero of Fort Blakely" relished and deserved the distinction of being a Civil War champion. Townspeople nicknamed the bearded war hero "Col. Busey." Some of the men who served under him now resided in Urbana.

Col. Busey selected those men. Those volunteers marched out of the line. He focused their efforts on tearing down the stables and small buildings north and northeast to check the further spread of fire. Some were armed with axes and hoes. Others simply used their hands to pry boards apart. They dismantled grayed strips of wood from a structure that could barely be called a house before it became kindling. At least three stables were hacked and chopped apart within five minutes.

Under the direction of Busey, the men created a successful firebreak.

Despite of the winds' push, the fire died before proceeding further east or north.

Whole burning brands, fiery embers, and flaming shingles drifted high in the air found nothing on which to feed its burning hunger.

The bucket brigade volunteers congratulated themselves in saving the homes on the north side of Green Street, between Race and Market. Each dwelling escaped smoke and fire damage.

Halberstadt and Busey heartily clapped the volunteers on the back.

Their self-congratulations were short-lived.

"Brenner's livery's aflame!" came a cry amid the surrounding fumes and heat.

The city councilmen and volunteers were so focused on the forward movement of the flames that they didn't notice how the wind retreated the air-borne kindling among the seething fire behind them.

Without hesitation, they rushed south to the Brenner paddock.

Half the brigade quickly cleared the livery of all animals and carriages. A third of them tossed buckets of water. The rest gathered pails to refill them.

Despite their best efforts, leaves and trees dried from nature's autumn kiss provided the tinder around the Brenner stables and home. A dried–out sycamore tree carried orange and yellow tongues of flame toward the newly painted porch.

"Wyatt!"

Earp instinctively turned to face the woman calling his name.

She ran into the arms of the ruddy-faced livery owner who was standing amid the smoke.

"Oh, Wyatt. So much lost to the fire," she wept in her husband's arms.

"Praise God all family survived," Brenner comforted his wife.

The Methodist Church on Race Street that unwittingly supplied the initial torching candle lay in the fire's path. Earp uncomfortably savored a subtle pleasure that the religious structure was threatened.

From the edge of the alley, Earp stood conflicted as the flames closed in on the thirty-year-old church, the first church built in Urbana. Taking a deep breath, he stamped out small flames around the lawn. Finally, he tipped over a half-empty rain barrel to squelch the ground sparks from spreading across the brown grass to the church.

Another Heaven-sent southwest wind shifted the flames to the church's coal house instead. A small stable on the Brenner homestead was sacrificed and consumed instead.

The other horse stalls blazed as did the house where the Brenners used to live. The family stood outside watching with a few belongings they gathered.

God saved His house, but not those of His congregation, Earp mused ruefully.

Shrugging his shoulders, he turned to head to work. He avoided the alley along the smoldering ruins of the widows' stables and homes. He advanced up Race Street past Green Street and the unburned homes on its north side.

With the threat of the bounty hunter removed, he could remain in Urbana and employed at the Boneyard Creek Social Club.

As Earp came to Elm Street, an overpowering sweet stench of pine chips stopped him in his tracks. Something was wrong in the lot next to where he was staying. A new plume of smoke spewed out of a house belonging to Tom Lindsey. He thought some tenant named Ireland was living there.

Earp charged past his house across the yard.

He yanked open the front door to see if it was occupied. The inside was lit up. Flames mushroomed up the walls and over chairs and tables.

"Hey, anyone here?" he shouted.

The arsonist popped his head from the other room. His gun appeared next. He torched the room by smashing a kerosene-filled hurricane lamp.

Earp dove from the front door. He rolled away from the burning structure.

From his new viewpoint, Earp saw the burning house was attached to two businesses, Denton and Lindsey's cabinet shop and Marty Kaucher's carpenter shop. Both contained prime tinder for fire. Wood shavings and oils just waiting to be ignited.

Both of those buildings were empty. Ireland, Denton, Lindsey, and Kaucher enlisted their aid to the bucket brigade.

Earp didn't know if the stranger knew that or he took advantage of the opportunity. Again, he had more questions than answers.

The arsonist came to the front door and aimed at Earp.

Earp looked the arsonist dead in the eye, almost daring him to shoot.

"Dad, the shop's on fire," screamed a young voice.

The arsonist evaded the boy's view by lunging back inside.

Earp looked. He recognized one of the boys who were playing in the Widow Shepherd stable. He stood at the corner of Race and Elm, the north lot of the untouched homes.

"Tommy. Get away from there!" shouted the paternal voice filled with fear and caution.

His young son grabbed a bucket to help. He ran off to find some water.

Moved by the boy's fearlessness, Earp stood up and searched the smoke for movement from the outside

A gunshot cracked. The dirt spit up near Earp's boots.

He jumped back and ran toward a smoldering stable.

The cacophony of the splashing of water, the mayor's yelling, walls and roofs collapsing, human voices mixed with animals' cries, and other discordant noises associated with fire-fighting blotted out the booming blast from a revolver.

Two more shots snapped from beside the burning shops.

Wood splintered twice on the paddock fence around the small stable. Earp ducked inside. There was only one stall and a dappled quarter horse was still in it. In the yard, a newly-painted green buckboard wagon remained unhitched.

Earp saddled the horse and hopped on it. The colt galloped out of the now-blazing stable. It sheltered behind the buckboard.

Earp peeked over the wagon at the majestic County Courthouse across the street. The three story brick structure loomed, daring the fire to approach. It rested in the middle of the block surrounded by thin trees and a leaf-cluttered park. No one was hiding among them.

He knew the County Jail was on the other side. He avoided any confrontation with Urbana's Police Division. At the whorehouse, law enforcement avoided him as much as he avoided them.

He looked across the alleyway at the house he rented. For the first time, he noticed fire through its bedroom window.

Maybe the stranger was a bounty hunter trying to burn him out, he thought. *But why didn't he take him back at the stables.*

Figures dashed from across the street.

Kaucher and his son ran toward the carpentry shop, but it was too late. It was enveloped in red and gold flares. More volunteers joined them to toss whatever water they had handy. They resisted boiling themselves alive as smoke stung their eyes and parched their throats.

The relentless brigade scoped out the fire as it spread to north side of Elm Street. From the woodworking shops, it surged along elms and oaks to a house owned by Frank and Mike Tiernan. Almost all the volunteers knew it was occupied by the Boneyard Creeks Social Club's bouncer. Despite the water, it consumed a stable on the same lot and the residences of lawyers named Webber and Alexander Spence.

Winds blew on the fire, making it swell. Immediately, the rear of the business block on Main Street overheated by the autumn sun and caught fire.

Halberstadt ordered a search for fresh sources of water. The initial resources were drying up as the fire wasn't abating. In fact, the empty wooden troughs and rain barrels provided additional kindling for the fire. Thatched well caps and roofs had already burned away.

More water was needed.

The wind increased.

The smoke increased.

More houses and more shops burned. Baked timber, saplings, shrubbery, and foliage provided more combustible nourishment. The fire line didn't distinguish between leaves or branches of elm, willow, maple, oak, or sycamore. The sweeping southwest winds encouraged its progeny closer and closer to Urbana's Main Street prosperous commerce.

By now, Twaddler finished his purloined pastry. Glancing out the café's window, he noticed that intermingled gray and black smoke sailed closer. Despite the late afternoon sun, he made out a distinctive reddish glow over the tall businesses, offices, and lodgings across the street. Stepping outside, he acknowledged the heat was much more oppressive then minutes earlier.

To his right, he saw what appeared to be a hundred men lined up along a block and a half on Race Street to Main Street, and a block along Main Street into a shallow Boneyard Creek.

Townsmen with shirts and trousers blackened by soot and burns assumed a well-practiced formation along the creek's bank filling metal pails. Sweating and muddy men formed a single-minded human chain of water from a stream dried up by the extended summerlike weather to a growing fire because of the same unusually hot autumn.

One row passed the creek's water to douse the flames as the other row exchanged empty buckets back. Tiernan Brother stood next to Busey Brother to hand filled pails. Brenner who lost his livery earlier continued to dispatch buckets. Marty Kaucher who lost his carpentry shop early never left the side of his fire-fighting comrades. His son, Tommy, assisted in any way possible. The boy revered every single member of the bucket brigade.

O. C. Cunningham, the principal of the grade and high school, commandeered a pack of stout young men down to the creek's hilly embankment. Under his stern instruction, they filled the pails with great efficiency. The water level was low from the warm, dry weather so to provide quicker refill. Cunningham ignored all decorum and respectability as he splashed in the creek passing out buckets of water.

Once again, Halberstadt shouted, "1, 2, 3, pour! 1, 2, 3, pour!"

Like before, three, four, five buckets were poured at a time onto the flames. Men handed the empty pails to men behind them. They passed buckets to other men who scooped water out of the creek. Filled buckets were again dumped to allow the men to advance on the fire.

In an attempt to stem the fire from downtown, Halberstadt realized a new rhythm was needed. Men were tiring. Men were yielding to despair and surrender. It was beginning to look like the fire couldn't be stopped. It grew in spite of the valiant efforts of the Urbana volunteers.

Now, Halberstadt directed two or three men to step forward to toss water. As they stepped back to hand off the empty bucket, two or three men stepped forward to unload. Exhaustion forced the two or three men to shift down the line. Refreshed men renewed their efforts in dousing the flames.

"1, 2, step, pour. Retreat. Sidestep of you need a break. 1, 2, step, pour. Retreat," Halberstadt's voice remained strong although his throat dried from the heat and overuse. School teacher Kristina Wein urged him on.

This method revived the bucket brigade's battle. The push was back on!

Twaddler considered his options. A sweltering gale made the decision for him as it pushed him east on Main Street away from the approaching inferno. It was as if he was being ushered to the whorehouse.

A block away, Earp squinted as his meager belongings went up in smoke. He didn't have much, so he wasn't overly concerned. He fretted about the money he had stashed in a hidden lockbox underneath the floorboards.

...refreshed men renewed their efforts.

He decided that he needed to track the stranger from setting more fires. He searched for any sign of the arsonist. The smoke stung his eyes making the pursuit more difficult but not impossible. He led the colt away from the oppressive heat to the near deserted Market Street.

Earp caught eye of Twaddler waddling toward him, but he wasn't alone.

Moments before, Twaddler had wandered into the arsonist's path.

After a gust propelled Twaddler east to Market Street, the armed stranger popped out from behind an elm tree and grabbed the drunk.

Threatening Twaddler by placing the heated barrel against his temple, the arsonist yelled at Earp, "Stop chasing me!"

Earp noticed the distinctive Southern twang that Twaddler mentioned. But like Twaddler, he couldn't identify from where in the South it originated.

"I thought you were after me."

"Now, why would I give a damn about some lowlife Yankee?"

"Why're you starting these here fires then?"

"Dang it. Nothing personal, y'all unnerstand. Y'all find out soon enough."

"Why Urbana?"

"Y'all ask a lot of questions."

"We can end this if'n you just let my friend go?"

"Your friend?" Twaddler and the stranger said at the same time.

"Shut your mouth," the arsonist spat as he jammed the barrel into Twaddler. It singed his earlobe.

"Owww!" Twaddler whined.

"Let him go. You can walk away," Earp offered.

"Can't walk away. Not until I finish my business here anyway," the stranger giggled.

"Business? What business?"

"The KKK. If you and your friend need to know. Here, Chicago, and a heap of other towns north of the Mason Dixon gonna burn."

"The Ku Klux Klan?"

"Damn right! You Yankees burn up Savanna, Atlanta. Call it retribution. We're doing retribution here."

"General Sherman's March to the Sea?"

"Your General Sherman! Damn him to Hell! May he join that cuss Lincoln there!"

Twaddler's eyes flared as did Earp's. Cursing Illinois' Favorite Son is not something native Illinoisans took lightly.

"Take him out now," Twaddler grimaced.

Earp aimed his revolver at the stranger.

"Want to take that chance?"

"Gimme the horse."

"Not mine to give."

"Don't care. Git off the horse and I'll let this rummy go."

Earp slid off the gray quarter horse, but kept the gun pointed at Twaddler's captor.

The arsonist shoved Twaddler into Earp. Both went down.

"The South will rise again!" He declared as he mounted the horse and fired a shot at the downed pair. He reared up the horse triumphantly.

Twaddler and Earp vaulted behind the scaly, brownish-gray trunk of a tree to avoid the charging hooves.

"This here's big news. Not going to waste time jawing with you two." The arsonist pulled the trigger a couple more times and he trotted north toward Main Street.

"Are you shot?" Earp asked as he saw blood near Twaddler.

"Nah. I think I cut my hand when I fell, friend. Go get that son-of-a-bitch. It hurts, but I'll live," Twaddler gritted his teeth as he clutched his hand to his chest smearing blood on his dirt-speckled shirt.

"Actually, I need you to get the girls out of the Social Club," Earp said as he yanked Twaddler up.

"The fire that bad?" Twaddler asked as Earp put his arm under the injured man's shoulder.

"No telling. If the fire gets past the railroad tracks, the woods are prime kindling. The brick building will become an oven and bake everyone inside. So if I'm going to stop that Rebel fool, I don't need to be worrying about the girls and Jane."

They stumbled to another stable near the rear of a two-story downtown tenement. Tiny orange flickers popped up on its weathered stable. A black stable nag, obviously a dray horse, whinnied in slowly rising panic.

"See that wagon over there," Earp nodded back to another stable now overrun by golden sparks. The new paint on the buckboard looked like it was steaming.

"Little help to hitch it up?" Twaddler said as he cast a wary eye to his wound.

"Haul your ass on the horse and I'll take care of the rest. I know where that Reb's headed."

A block west, the god-fearing bucket brigade helplessly witnessed wind, wood, and flame summon a scorching fire devil. The red-orange-yellow swirl meandered to engulf downtown. The blazing hurricane drew in smoke and gave off a hot scent of burnt wood and plaster.

From one end, Halberstadt reformed the squad from the ravaged buildings and desiccated lots along Race Street to Main Street. Busey yelled directions in concert from the middle of Main Street.

The volunteer brigade fought the flames along the west end of the two-story block on the south side of Main Street. Yellow and orange blazes lit up several of the shops on the lower level.

"Everything's burning in my bakery," moaned Al Spence as he hoisted a full pail of water. His provision store was less a concern to him. It was insured.

"Same with my harnesses, Spence," said J.C. Gilliand as he took the empty bucket from the baker. "At least, we're not Eppstein."

No one bothered Samuel Eppstein as he just stood in front of his blazing cigar store. He recently re-opened after moving there from across the street. He had to relocate because of a fire back in June. He inhaled the mixture of sweet tobaccos. He wasn't sure if insurance would cover this so soon after.

"All my pipes. Choice cigars, Havanna cigars, fine tobacco," he sounded like one of his newspaper advertisements. "Everything up in smoke," his voice cracked. No one laughed at his unintentional pun.

Determined flames pushed firebrands airborne to the north side. Both sides of Main Street took fire from Spence's block when conflagration was at its hottest.

Busey put his hands on Halberstadt's shoulder and leaned close to whisper.

"If these men can't stop the blaze before Water Street, it'll cross over into the lumber yard then over the tracks. Then the dry woods will spread the fire across the county," he confided to his mayor.

Halberstadt was aware of the imminent disaster and he looked woefully upon the brave citizens of Urbana.

Two tiers of volunteers felt like they were standing inside a two-story, block wide fireplace. Sour sweat and acrid charring intermingled to bite nostrils from the inside. Hair was singed with shirts and trousers.

The families living in the upper floors escaped with whatever household items they could carry.

Some discouraged men broke from the bucket brigade to join the women and children rescue the merchandise from stores.

The block had survived for twenty years. It encompassed five statuesque tenements. However, it would not endure another day.

Black-haired, well-dressed John Gere tried to force the remaining volunteers to focus on his property, the first and second tenement.

In the second tenement, his dry goods store occupied the entire lower level. On the upper floor, a law office conducted business in the front and Miss Crissey operated her hat shop in the back until that day.

Water tossed on the third building tried to rescue H. M. Russell's law office and a provision store owned by the Burt Brothers. Russell and the brothers were also among the loyal bucket brigade members. Russell had a strong chin but weak eyes. Last week, he purchased his fancy new spectacles from Burt & Burt.

Such were the thoughts as bucket after bucket was emptied and refilled and emptied and refilled and emptied.

Several blocks east, Twaddler drove the horse and wagon further north on Main Street. As soon as he crossed the railroad track, he shouted and screamed as he pulled up to the whorehouse.

"Git your asses out here," Twaddler screamed.

"Go sleep it off, you lush," was the faceless response.

"Blackie sent me. Now git out here, you damn fools."

Madame Jane unshuttered the upper floor window and stuck out her head. "Who you calling a damn fool, you damn fool?"

"You smell that? And that ain't fluffy clouds floating close to your window!"

"Lordie!" Madame Jane shrieked. "Where's them water bucket men?"

"Them's doing their best. But Blackie wants you and the rest of the girls out of harm's way just in case! Now, haul ass!"

Something in Twaddler's tone was not to be argued with. Madame Jane responded by shouting orders of her own not to be trifled with.

Soon, all the working girls were loaded in the wobbly buckboard with Madame Jane next to Twaddler. They were dressed in various stage of dress. Their breasts and asses were covered and that's all Twaddler could hope for.

With one eye closed, Madame Jane stared down Twaddler.

"Blackie sent you? Why ain't he here hisself?"

"He's fighting the fire in his own way. Don't you mind!"

Twaddler had dropped his friend off on the northwest corner of Market and Main Streets on his way to the Social Club.

As soon as Earp jumped off, he took note of the stolen quarter horse eating the dry grass on the Court House lawn. In the middle of the street, some crates filled with metal rollers and platens lay next tow some burnt newsprint and spilled black ink.

He realized that Frank Snyder of the Republican saved them from the upper floor where the Urbana Republican was printed and published.

He sprinted up the stairs two steps at a time. Snyder was at the top struggling to hold two cases of heavy leaden type. Not moving, Snyder was arguing with someone in his office.

"Frank. I'm here to help," Earp whispered. He slowly ascended the last couple of stairs.

"I travelled here to burn this here town where Lincoln was born."

"President Lincoln wasn't born here. In fact, he never even lived here," Snyder shot back. He had been listening to this goof ramble on for nearly quarter of an hour.

"Lying Yankee. The Klan is getting revenge for Sherman's March!"

"No way I'm gonna print anything like a lie like that."

"Shouldda known no paper named the Republican won't never write something about the Klan's patriotic mission."

"We've been reporting on how Grant and Congress be trying to put the Klan out of business."

"Those damn fool laws. Taking away our individual rights."

"You're inciting violence."

"For months, Klan members been planning this attack. We got our people planted in Chicago, Wisconsin, and Michigan. Setting fires and getting revenge."

"Nothing's been reported."

"Dang it. We just started it yesterday. I rode here all night. Someone tol' me it was closer than it was. I was suppose to burn this here town starting last night. But I wuz tol' it was a couple hours ride."

"Whoever told you that was wrong. Just like you thinking Lincoln was born around here."

"Stall him," whispered Earp. "Is there a back door?"

"Hey, is anything of that true?" Snyder pressed. "I need to know your name for the record. I'll need to get my notebook. It's on my desk by the rear door."

Earp quietly slid out his revolver out and edged a step down.

"Nothing doing, Yankee. Y'all get my name when I'm safe and sound back home. My name and everyone else's name. We'll be famous. We'll be heroes. All I gotta do is finish burning this here town to the ground."

Earp paused as he listened to the sound of glass shattering and a whoosh.

"Noooo!" screamed Snyder. "Blackie, do something!"

By the time Earp got to the top of the stairs, he saw the arsonist smashing oil lamps amid newsprint and on wooden desks crowded in the office.

"You keep saving your equipment," Earp told a white-face Snyder. "I'll take care of him."

Earp targeted the arsonist.

"Hold it right there."

The arsonist shouted with his back turned to Earp. "Damn you, Yankee. I knew I shouldda shooed that horse way off." In one movement, he pulled out his gun and spun around. He fired a shot at Earp.

It missed, of course.

Earp dodged the bullet in time but his ears rang from such a violent bang inside an enclosed space.

He made sure that Snyder wasn't shot. The gray-haired publisher/reporter wasn't there.

Snyder dashed down and had just returned up the stairs to continue removing his reporter notebooks and printing supplies away from the encroaching heat and fire.

Earp aimed his gun at the arsonist who was now hiding behind a large oaken desk where Snyder wrote his stories and managed the newspaper.

He pulled the trigger and the paper on Snyder's desk scattered. The air grew torrid. The smoke congealed.

Earp looked for the rear exit.

Standing in the doorway, he whispered to Synder who was grabbing another box.

"Any other way out?"

"Just the double doors like I said. Newsprint gets delivered through the back," Snyder wheezed. The smoke solidified any breathable air.

Earp swore and ducked into the office. Small fires flared here and there, but nothing the bucket brigade couldn't handle.

The arsonist fired another shot.

Earp couldn't see where he was. Although his ears still buzzed, he heard Snyder shuffling behind him. He took another shot, hoping his foe would reveal himself.

Only response was another gunshot fired at him. A counter top splintered on a nearby desk.

The gunshot jangled his nerves because of the high-pitched ringing in his ears, but he heard Snyder topple to the floor behind him. He wondered if a bullet found the newspaperman.

Then his hearing returned as he detected erratic, staccato hacking in the newspaper office. Fire spat and dripped from the rafters.

A flash of light popped from the rear.

Earp rushed toward it. As he approached, he saw the rear double doors burst open wide and fresh air rushed in as cloudy smoke poured out. But only for a moment. Wind, or the arsonist's foot, forced the double doors shut just as quick.

The arsonist was making his escape.

Earp had no choice, but to blindly run out the doors to try and stop him.

He kicked the door to slam it open. He propelled himself outside.

A bullet erupted from the street below.

The side of one door cracked against the wooden railing.

Earp crouched in anticipation.

The Klansman swore and fired again.

This time Earp fired immediately in response and toward the gunshot. He nailed his Southern outlaw in the middle of his forehead.

The unnamed arsonist growled as he keeled over at the bottom of the steps. Earp would never learn the man's name.

He wheeled around back into the newspaper office.

Now most of the office and press room in flames. The fire flickered like a yellow and red mushroom. The ceiling trickled flames like drops of red-orange water. The printing presses and the remaining newspaper material were lost. Snyder lay on the floor not moving. In trying to save his property, the exertion and smoke proved to be too much for aging journalist. Snyder had chosen to sacrifice his life in trying to save his sole purpose for living.

Earp grabbed the man. He detected shallow breathing. Relieved, he hauled the unconscious Snyder up by his arms and dragged him to the hallway.

Nearly roasted alive, Earp barely survived the dense fumes himself. He struggled to maneuver the steps that suddenly felt to be longer and steeper.

Then, unexpected help arrived.

The sandy-haired man that Snyder was arguing with earlier appeared at Earp's side. They carried Snyder beyond danger.

As they carried Snyder down the stairs and out into the street, Earp's head began to clear.

"We would have been lost if not for you," he croaked.

"Snyder's one of the best journalists I know. I hate to see anything happen to him. I came to help him," the sandy-haired reporter said.

As Earp and the reporter lugged Snyder further away from the burning building, Twaddler rode up Market Street with the wagon load of women.

Earp breathed easier because he breathed clearer air outside and he saw his Boneyard Creek Social Club charges were unharmed.

Instances of heroic labor and unselfish devotion to the work of assisting the unfortunates are abundant to contrast the actions of cowardice and recusancy.

Weakened from the oppressive heat and noxious fumes, Earp dropped to one knee. He inhaled deeply. He was reduced to being a mere spectator to the diversity of the human condition in the middle of inhuman catastrophe.

Men, women, and children raced in and out of downtown shops. Some rescued provisions like harnesses, dresses, shirts, hats, rocking chairs, serving dishes, shovels, and the like. Others stole a variety of merchandise from the same shops and ran off.

Some dared the flames and were burned. Others remained untouched.

Men with wagons offered aid.

Some obeyed the slightest command from Halberstandt and Busey. Others refused to submit to their well-intentioned authority.

At this, as in all such calamities, gallant fellows challenged the oncoming disaster while insubordinate loafers utterly offer assistance.

Most men unhesitatingly put aside differences to render aid. Others took advantage of the situation.

A few men who realized the fire destroyed their financial obligations stopped assisting the fire brigade. A brawny malingerer in patched brown overalls led the taunts.

"Let it burn," he jeered.

"Yeah, there's goes my bills," heckled another.

"Gilliand, your ledgers are gone. So is my debt."

"No more IOUs for me!"

"No more overdraft."

"I guess my expenses are wiped clean."

"My credit is good again."

"Whatever I owed at the Burt store are ashes now!"

Madame Jane shouted, "Hold those horses, Twaddler."

Twaddler yanked back on the reins.

"Whatssa matter, Jane?"

"That's Madame Jane to you."

"It's Edmund to you," he grunted in response.

"Why are those men just standing there and not helping?"

"If you stop flapping your jaw, you'd know the fire is wiping out their notes they owe on. Now, let's get out of here."

"Girls, heave off."

"What?"

"It's time to do our part!"

The wanton women considered her words with scrunched up faces.

"Grab a bucket and lend a hand. Let's show those slackers what it means to fight a fire!"

The tarts whooped it up and sprung off the wagon. They got in line. Other townswomen soon joined in. Inspired by the less-than-pure working girls, many ladies, including school teacher Wein, took a place along the bucket brigade and rendered material assistance. Soon, Halberstadt saw his Rebecca taking an empty bucket from one scantily clad girl and passing back to another painted lady. He couldn't have been prouder of his better half. Even the hatmaker Miss Crissey joined in the efforts to save the town when her own business lay in ashes.

"1, 2, step, pour. Retreat. Sidestep if you need a break. 1, 2, step, pour. Retreat," Halberstadt's tone was reinvigorated by the sight of his wife.

Again two or three men stepped forward to toss buckets of water. As they receded to transfer the empty buckets, two or three men advanced to deliver the water.

The feminine influence revived the bucket brigade's battle. Men instinctively sought to impress the women. The additional aid lightened their load as well.

The push was back on!

Eventually, the men who heckled the bucket brigade dispersed. The womenfolk shamed them.

Twaddler saw his friend, Blackie, by another man holding an unconscious

Madame Jane shouted, "Hold those horses, Twaddler."

man in the middle of Main Street.

He climbed off the wagon to help.

"Let's load him aboard and help the volunteers," Twaddler suggested.

The sandy-haired man said, "I got this. You go lend a hand to put out the fire."

As the sandy-haired man dragged Snyder off, Twaddler lifted Earp to his feet.

"We've got another problem," Earp gasped for air as he pointed to the deceased arsonist at the side of the now-charred building.

"Blackie, we've got to get him out of here. It'll raise too many nasty questions," Twaddler added.

"I shot him in self-defense. Throw him on the back of that wagon and take him to the constable's."

"Every man of the department's joined the bucket brigade, Blackie. Toss his worthless ass in the wagon. We can worry about it later."

Earp and Twaddler hoisted and callously tossed the dead body over the buckboard side as Twaddler crawled back into the wagon seat.

Brenner wife's summoned her husband. "Wyatt. I'm here to help."

Earp again instinctively jerked his head toward the woman.

Brenner shouted, "Git home to the youngins', woman."

"Wyatt, thems helping at the creek with Principal Cunningham."

Earp twitched at hearing his real name being called again.

"Move aside, Wyatt," Brenner's wife demanded and her husband welcomed her by his side.

Twaddler cleared his throat. "You gonna join the bucket brigade, Blackie?"

"No, I seen another problem I need to take care of first."

Twaddler headed north then west on Water Street, a block north of downtown. He knew more much help was needed as much as it galled him.

Other water buckets focused on the fourth tenement. The owner, J. W. Shuck, yet another lawyer, worked on the lower half. His tenants, Heisler & Coler Hardware, sold in the front and Sheldon and Jaques had law offices in the back. It looked like he was going to lose their tenancy despite his efforts.

The remaining bucket brigade, reinforced by the feminine aspect of the town, tried to conquer the fire on the fifth building that housed A. O. Clapp's drug store. The ever-expanding fire claimed still more law offices.

The next building, a mere fifteen years old was once occupied by the Grand Prairie Bank. It now consisted of two tenements, the eastern being owned by W. H. Somers and J. O. Cunningham. The western portion was Shuck and Hollister's Main Street Café, with another set of doomed law offices.

Next door, the provision store, also owned and operated by the partnership of Shuck & Hollister, resided on the lower floor. Above now were the smoking remains of Snyder's Republican newspaper.

One shady-looking wagoneer patched brown overalls filled his horse-drawn buckboard with a load of valuable merchandise from Shuck & Hollister's store. He assisted the business in saving the unburned goods. After he rode off, he reconsidered his kind offer. When he realized he wasn't being watched, he attempted to escape into the wooded countryside. As the brawny fellow crossed northern railroad tracks, he felt a cold barrel of a gun against the back of his neck.

"Turn this wagon around, mister," Earp said

"Wha?"

"Noticed you bragging about your unpaid debts to Shuck & Hollister's. I kind of got suspicious when you offered to haul their goods to safety. You don't have the look of an honest man."

"Awww, Blackie, I was only joshing," the ruddy-face wagoneer choked on his own lies.

The disgruntled driver turned his horse to the south side where Shuck and Hollister were taking inventory.

At the same time, Twaddler halted his "borrowed" wagon midway between Urbana and Champaign. He backed into the woods near Boneyard Creek where he seen coyotes and foxes linger. He dropped the rear gate and kicked out the stinking corpse into a shriveled copse.

"No better than you deserve," Twaddler eulogized and he heaved the gate back up. "Hope the critters don't choke on you."

He figured if anyone discovered bones later, it would only add to the creek's legend.

Then Twaddler breathed in deep. He sucked in the crisp afternoon air and his pride. He forced the horse into the town of Champaign.

Like Twaddler himself, the animal had a natural revulsion to entering the detested terrain.

Twaddler hadn't been journeyed there since his wife ran off.

After dropping off the nearly stolen merchandise, Earp persuaded the wagoneer to reluctantly return to "assist" other shop owners.

"Damn, Blackie, look at what's left."

"It's not even five o'clock and nothing's left from here to Main Street 'cept that row of houses on Green Street," Earp added.

They surveyed the blacked stumps and smoldering ruins of houses and stables. Thin wisps of smoke floated around the wagon wheels.

"I used to live over there," Earp tried to finish, but a whiff of scorched lumber filled his nostrils and reddened his eyes again.

The brawny wagoneer in the patched overalls knocked Earp off. He urged his horse to gallop away from Urbana that night.

Humiliated, he shouted, "I don't want to put my horse and wagon in any more danger."

Earp expected nothing less from the man. Urbana was well rid of the shameful bastard.

He listened to the sizzles and crackle of dying embers surround him as the frantic commotion on the other side of Main Street surged.

Simmering heat reminded Earp of the recent damage. He noticed his singed hair and moustache for the first time. He smelled of smoke and horse.

A blast of feverish air wrapped around him as Earp joined Halberstadt in the middle of the street.

"Where do you need me?"

"We got to conquer this fire soon, Blackie!" Halberstadt shouted amid the roar of the fire's consumption of the sidewalk planks and storefronts.

"What about that western tenement?" Earp stared at the burgeoning flames to his right.

"Ermentrout and Harvey's bank. Grant and Lindsey's harness shop just above them."

"A lot of them household furniture, tables and beds, and what-not were saved, but still damaged somewhat," Earp shouted to get the mayor's attention.

The mayor worried as the two-story frame structure, immediately west was a owned by Frederick. Eubeling. The mayor knew his father, Alexander, well. Eubeling was a genius with making and repairing boots and shoes. His friend's buildings were about to be destroyed.

"Of course, all was in hurry and confusion and in too many cases no care was used," Halberstadt regretted.

In Champaign, Twaddler trotted half a mile and clambered down from the bench. His hand ached as his heart beat faster. He bled a little more as he pounded on the door to a single story house.

It was a nice house, he thought.

The door opened and for the first time in years Edmund Twaddler was face-to-face with Mary, his ex-wife.

He couldn't believe the internal feelings he experienced toward her.

Back in Urbana, Busey joined Earp and Halberstadt.

"Mr. Mayor. The fire's fast approaching the town limits," Busey screamed bringing the mayor back into focus. His brown beard was blackened and his cheeks scalded.

Shaking off his despair, Halberstadt's eyes bored sharply into Earp's.

"Just beyond the northern corporate limits, there're acres and acres of dry, virgin timber just," Halberstadt's voice cracked. "Just the other side of those railroad tracks. If we can't stop it before the fire reaches the lumber yard and that farming warehouse on Water Street, the fire will cross over wipe out all the woods north of here. And quite possibly will spread to other towns."

Earp asked, "How much land?"

"At least half of Champaign County. At least," Halberstadt choked.

Bringing the mayor and the whorehouse bouncer back to the immediate situation, Busey stated, "Most of the smaller merchandise like watches, jewelry, clocks, and even spectacles, most still in cases were partly saved."

"What about Heisler and Coler?" Halberstadt asked.

"Nothing of their stock saved," Busey reported.

More than half the stock on Main Street was removed beyond the threat of the fire's further spread.

Earp added, "Some of the stock may be unburned but stolen. Unsupervised removal made it easy for thieves and shop lifters to steal."

"Constables and deputies are needed to fight the fire, not prevent theft," the mayor explained.

Earp, as Blackie, halted any further thefts as police officers were occupied in the bucket brigade line.

The bucket brigade, now with men and women in scorched clothing and singed hair, handed buckets back and forth with machine like movements. Battling the flames and heat, they hauled water and empty pails like well-oiled pistons in an assembly line from the creek.

The volunteers doused the entire north side of Main Street to prevent the fire spreading to the two story wooden agricultural warehouse. However, it was destroyed as well as the adjacent residences of John Gere and James Porter. Gere and Porter ignored the loss and continued to retrieve empty buckets from the front line.

Part of the brick block on the north side was burning. Down the street, the new block of Busey Brothers, Gill & Burt, part of which is occupied by the Gazette job office and bindery was seriously endangered.

The last hope of resistance crumbled as the large stock of lumber in the Webster, Davies, and Co. Yard, ignited by falling sparks and fiery debris like tree branches and shingles..

Boneyward Creek still flowed, but the water bearers were tiring and soaked to the skin.

Principal Cunningham was coughing and wheezing as he struggled to fill the pails. His students struggled to keep up with the demand for more water.

Even Cunningham felt like his efforts were fruitless. Despaired, he kneeled in the creek and prayed.

His prayers were interrupted by the short, quick clanging of a brass bell that peeled from above on the bridge.

Twaddler was hanging on a fire steam pumper jangling the bell's clapper. A fire pump steamer arrived with a team of horses and a full complement of fire-fighters. Every townsfolk couldn't believe what they read on the side of the fire engine - Champaign Fire Co. 2. The red and gold trimmed wheels, four-foot high, carried an enormous copper vat and canvass hoses.

The Urbana volunteers, with faith in humanity restored, found new strength to battle the blaze.

Urbana to a man and woman acknowledged sincere gratitude for the timely and effective assistance rendered by Champaign and its gallant firemen. Soon, several more of Champaign citizens crossed the bridge to replace the exhausted bucket brigade members.

The officers of the Fire Company aided by the bucket lines of citizens saved further loss. The fire was completed extinguished in minutes and yards from the wooded forest north of the tracks.

The threat of fire was removed. Flames never crossed the railroad tracks. The woods were allowed to follow its natural cycle of death and rebirth without cataclysmic interference.

Tommy Kaucher studied their every move with hero worship in his eyes.

When the fire was over, an I. B. & W. Railroad executive formally invited the bucket brigade, men and women, along with the men of the Champaign Fire Department to accept a generous luncheon that was prepared at the Griggs House. At the exquisitely-designed Italianate house, the guests of hone congregated and partook with hearty appetites stoked from battling fire for several hours.

Urbana townsfolk and Champaign fire fighters jointly celebrated the victory at the Griggs House. Attendees were honored to enter the dwelling with its decorated cornices and projecting bay on the east side. The magnificent front porch heralded a balustrade and is supported by bracketed columns and presented a glorious entrance for the town heroes.

The Gazette reporter, the sandy-haired man, announced that he could faithfully report that any feelings of rivalry on both sides wiped out and forgotten on the common efforts to save life and property.

At the close of the feast, short speeches by town council members sincerely expressed testimonials of brotherly love and an empathic desire to dissolve any bitter antagonism between the neighboring towns.

Halberstadt graciously declined to join in the speech making. He chose to rest his throat which was raw from yelling orders for the last few hours.

Although they shared the sentiments being expressed, Urbana and Champaign citizens alike soon tired of the stuff shirts pontificating the same praise with different words over and over.

Amidst the hearty cheers for various parties who took a prominent part in quelling the flames, the party broke up.

Before the autumn sun set on that Monday evening, the fire engine men reeled up their hoses. They prepared to ramble home with the horses leading the machinery with a sense of glory in saving the day.

The town fathers decided that now was not the time to estimate the loss sustained. Clearly, thirty buildings lie in ruins, but the two newly built brick opera halls in the downtown area survived, Busey's Hall and the Tiernan Building.

Much to the dismay of the slackers and hecklers, more than a few of the safes survived and were opened with ledgers, bills of sales, and accounts intact.

One triumph they applauded was that no life was lost.

Upon hearing that, Earp excused himself.

He wandered outside with his flask. He tipped it until it was empty.

Twaddler soon joined his friend outside.

"What you thinking about, Blackie?"

"It's time to move on. 'No life was lost.' That's going to raise some questions about me," Earp spoke without looking at Twaddler.

"I told you. I took care of him, Blackie. You've nothing to worry about. He got exactly what he deserved. No one will ask about what happened to him," Twaddler promised confidently.

"I'm heading west."

"Don't you have work tonight? Was The Boneyard Social Club damaged?"

Earp chuckled for the second time in twentypfour hours.

"First time I think I ever heard you laugh, Blackie."

"The Boneyard Creek Social Club is completely untouched. Madame Jane gave everyone the night off. The girls were exhausted from their fire-fighting work. I think a couple of them're rehashing the choice of employment because of it."

"What you going do out west that you can't do here?" Twaddler asked as he sipped his unadulterated mug of coffee.

"Hunt buffalo," Earp said with a grin and chuckled for a third time.

"You gonna keep using the name John Black or go back to Wyatt Earp."

Earp paused. He stopped grinning.

"You mentioned it one night when we were imbibing heavily. Plus I saw you turn your head when Brenner's wife called to her husband."

"Maybe I should clear my name in Peoria afore heading out west." Earp changed the subject. "What made you think of getting Champaign Fire Department? I thought you hated them."

Taking the hint, Twaddler allowed it.

"I do. I did. Especially since my wife ran off with one of them fire department fellows. I was pretty bitter about it for the longest time. Then when I saw her tonight I couldn't believe how I felt."

"Pretty angry, I imagine."

"Not at all. I felt nothing. Not one iota. Not one speck of feeling at all. I couldn't believe it. I didn't give a hang about her. I was only thinking about the town, the people here. I was worried about Madame Jane and the girls. I gave no thought to her. I went there to ask her man for help. Don't hate him no more. Actually kind of feel sorry for him now. Turns out he's a good man. Didn't hesitate to get his crew together and rush over here. Just in time it seems."

"Things were getting pretty desperate," Earp acknowledged. "So you got absolutely no feelings for the woman who was once your wife?"

"Yep," he said. He looked hard at Earp. "Got no use for holding on to that kind of bitterness. It was holding corked me inside a bottle."

Earp took the hint, but knew he was going to ponder that at a later time in a different place. He changed the subject again.

"What you planning on doing? I noticed you drinking coffee that doesn't smell like whiskey."

"I reckon there's an opening of steady employment at the Boneyard Creek Social Club. That's where my affections lay now. Madame Jane cuts a fine figure of a woman."

"That she does," Earp agreed. "I reckon after tonight the bitterness between you two is eased up some. Yep, a lot of bitterness is healed over, I reckon."

After the celebration, Earp recovered the lockbox with his savings intact. The small tin lockbox like the downtown safes survived the Great Urbana Fire of 1871.

Earp was gone two days later when the Champaign County Gazette reported about another great fire in Chicago. However, it did not report on the devastating one in Peshtigo, Wisconsin, or the three other massive ones in Michigan.

In the Gazette's article about the "fearful conflagration in Urbana," the reporter ended with a note that "an empathic desire announced to make what had been two rivals and contentious really one – one in fact, as well as one in spirit and interest."

THE END

A BIT OF SURPRISE HISTORY

Growing up in Illinois, one cannot refer to Urbana or Champaign separately. It is Champaign-Urbana. I, like everyone else, thought it was because the University of Illinois was located there. But the newspaper account reported that the Great Fire of 1871 united the two previously rival towns.

In researching and writing *The Great Chicago Fire Conspiracy*[1], I learned about the four other fires that occurred at the exact time as the Great Chicago Fire. Then I read a brief mention of this "Great" fire in Urbana that occurred the day after the Great Chicago Fire started.

I thought the idea that blaming a cow for starting a massive fire was ridiculous. Then I read a newspaper account that the Urbana fire was caused by "two unidentified boys were playfully burning the legs off of bugs." And I thought how bizarre is that?

Lastly, I stumbled onto the fact that Wyatt Earp was not only in Illinois but near Urbana in 1871. When I discovered that Earp had escaped from a Peoria jail a few months before the fire, I knew there was a story to be told.

History is so much more compelling when presented as pulp fiction! Much thanks to The Urbana Free Library for providing archived newspaper articles.

GEORGE TACKES - After graduating college with an English degree in 1983, George wrote plays in the 1980s that were performed at Chicago theaters. From 1990s, he was a newspaper reporter for suburban newspapers.In the early 2000s, he worked as an associate editor for trade publications. In 2018, George attended his first Windy City Pulp and Paper Convention and got the pulp bug. Besides *The Great Chicago Fire Conspiracy*, Airship 27 has published his stories in *Sherlock Holmes: Consulting Detective Vol. 17* and *Domino Lady Vol. 5*.[1]

1　Available from Airship 27 Productions via Amazon: airship27hangar.com for details.

THE WILD WEST

After the bloody American Civil War ended, the rugged landscape that was the frontier west was soon flooded with all manner of immigrants: from cowboys, pioneer settlers and all manner of outlaws. In their path were the various Indian tribes desperate to save their way of life. Soon the mountains, plains and valleys echoed with the sounds of gunfire and bloodshed flowed like rivers in these lawless territories.

A rare breed of men took on the challenge of bringing justice the west. Men like the Mysterious Masked Rider, the Earp brothers, and Wild Bill Hickock in tales from today's best New Pulp writers!

It's time to saddle up, pulp readers, for classic western action as only the Masked Rider can deliver.

PULP FICTION FOR A NEW GENERATION!

FOR AVAILABILITY OF THIS AND OTHER FINE READING GO TO
AIRSHIP27HANGAR.COM

AN AIRSHIP 27 PRODUCTION

Airship 27 Productions

NEW PULP

www.ingramcontent.com/pod-product-compliance
Lightning Source LLC
Chambersburg PA
CBHW051139260626

47170CB00005B/1886